Wined and Died. Book 8 of ... *ded in Provence Mysteries.* Copyright © 2018 by ... reserved.

Books by ...
The Magg...

Murder in the ...
Murder à la Carte
Murder in Provence
Murder in Paris
Murder in Aix
Murder in Nice
Murder in the Latin Quarter
Murder in the Abbey
Murder in the Bistro
Murder in Cannes
Murder in Grenoble
Murder in the Vineyard
Murder in Arles
A Provençal Christmas: A Short Story

The Stranded in Provence Mysteries
Parlez-Vous Murder?
Crime and Croissants
Accent on Murder
A Bad Éclair Day
Croak, Monsieur!
Death du Jour
Murder Très Gauche
Wined and Died
A French Country Christmas

The Irish End Games

Free Falling
Going Gone
Heading Home
Blind Sided
Rising Tides
Cold Comfort
Never Never
Wit's End
Dead On
White Out
Black Out

The Mia Kazmaroff Mysteries
Reckless
Shameless
Breathless
Heartless
Clueless
Ruthless

Ella Out of Time
Swept Away
Carried Away
Stolen Away

The French Women's Diet

WINED AND DIED

BOOK 8 OF THE STRANDED IN PROVENCE MYSTERIES

SUSAN KIERNAN-LEWIS

1

THERE OUGHTA BE A LAW

I'm trying to remember if I've ever worn handcuffs before.

I'm not surprised to discover that they are every bit as uncomfortable as I imagined.

But the thing that's even worse than the physical discomfort of having heavy cold steel clamped to your wrists is the humiliation of having them clamped to your wrists in front of the whole world to see.

This is what I was thinking as Eloise Basile marched me into the police *municipale* ahead of the two ninety-four year twin sisters I live with and also a good fourth of the population of the village of Chabanel where I live in southern France.

I think I was trying to focus my thoughts on something as mundane and banal as what it feels like to be handcuffed in order to better tune out the hullabaloo of the aforementioned people yelling either for my head or my release—all the while knowing that nothing anyone shouted was going to make a bit of difference one way or the other.

"Everyone knows why you are doing this, Mademoiselle

Basile," Léa Cazaly, one of the elderly twins shouted. "It is as obvious as your own shame."

"I'm doing it because the evidence tells me to," Eloise said, her face flushing with fury.

"You are doing it because you are angry with Marco but him you cannot touch," the other twin Justine interjected, referring to the man the three of us live with—who also happens to be Eloise's ex-boyfriend.

Eloise gave me a sharp push with her baton and I stumbled down the hall of the police station until I came to a set of two cells. The twins, or *les soeurs* as they are known in the village, were right behind us.

"Chief DeBray will be informed of this!" Léa said as Eloise finally unlocked the cuffs and pushed me into a cell.

Eloise slammed the cell door shut with an ominous clang.

"Even Chief DeBray does not condone murder!" she snarled at the twins.

As soon as Eloise spoke I saw she regretted her words. I know she wouldn't relent and release me, but I also know that Eloise was no fool when it comes to *les soeurs*.

She did *not* want to end up on their *merde* list.

"Do not worry, Jules," Justine said, patting my hand through the bars. "We will get this sorted out."

I nodded, feeling more than a little sick as I watched Eloise usher the twins back down the hall, leaving me in solitude and darkness, my stomach roiling.

I guess I should back up a little to explain how I got here.

2

TWENTY-FOUR HOURS EARLIER

I assume you're up on all the relevant details about me? How I came to France after being unceremoniously released from my emotional and contractual obligations from my almost-fiancé Gilbert? (In other words, I got dumped.) And how I then ended up stranded here in southern France—Provence to be precise—after a dirty bomb detonated over the Riviera and shut down all international travel not to mention working electronics and communication for the foreseeable future?

So are we all on the same page?

My current trouble began on a gorgeous October morning the day before a much-anticipated village harvest festival. The whole village of Chabanel was beside itself with excitement about this year's grape harvest. It seemed that this particular year there was just enough rain, plenty of sunshine, and no blights to deal with.

Now I should mention that Chabanel is like most little French villages in that it uses any excuse under the sun to throw a party and parade through the streets—usually in costume led by someone carrying a wooden idol of some long-forgotten saint. So the fact that everyone around these parts had a good grape harvest—*translation: no shortage of wine this year!*—was definitely reason to celebrate.

The upcoming harvest festival, or as *les soeurs* call it, *fête de la moisson* would be yet another opportunity to celebrate as a community but unlike most of our excuses to drink too much and dance 'til we're blue in the feet, this festival was to be held in one of the adjoining vineyards.

The particular field venue was chosen not so much because it had grown a good crop of grapes this year but because it was the closest to the town and the farmer who owned it didn't mind his field getting trampled and trashed.

As amazing as the weather is in the south of France in autumn, unfortunately it also means I was fighting terrible allergies all the time. There was something about the air in this part of the country during this time of year that just does a number on my sinuses. While it's possible to get Claritan on the black market it's not easy.

Plus the sisters tend to think purchasing medicine of any kind through the black market is illegal, immoral, and tantamount to throwing away good money when you could be using the black market for wine, chocolate, and truffles.

You know, the important things.

Instead, Justine had given me a set of my very own monogrammed handkerchiefs which was pretty much the extent of the twins' interest in how I dealt with my sneezing and sniffling.

In my other life back home in the US—Atlanta to be specific—I was a journalist as well as an equestrian. I mention the fact about horses because I own a horse here in France which is how I move about the countryside now that there are no more or very few operating cars.

My horse—who I wouldn't have paid five hundred bucks

for back in the US—is a steady, sound and generally agreeable animal whom I'm grateful beyond measure to have. He still throws me at least once every couple of weeks (he literally shies at his own shadow) but it's still better than the foot blisters I'd get walking the three-mile distance back and forth to the village from where I live in the country.

While it's true the aforementioned dirty bomb produced the EMP that affected all of Europe such that we in France no longer have cars, electricity, electronics or anything that used to operate using those things, in spite of what you might imagine, life has actually gotten better in the past three plus years. At least for me. Not because there have been any improvements in our destroyed infrastructure but because we've all gotten good at doing without.

Unlikely but valuable partnerships have sprung up that would have seemed impossible before all the lights were on.

Case in point is the fact that I now live with Léa and Justine as well as a young homeless guy with a twinkle in his eye and gold in his heart. Not that the homeless guy—who is, granted, no longer homeless since he lives with me and *les soeurs*—and I are together in any real sense. We're not.

Well, not unless you count the fact that we're legally married which he and I definitely try not to.

The other person who tries not to count that fact is my boyfriend Luc DeBray, the village chief of police.

Again, in normal times I might have seen Luc as a little stiff and formal for me but he's sexy as all get out and I have to say where he's short on chill and good-natured fun, he's long on honor and respect. You know, the boring stuff.

And *that, mes amis*, is an awesome trade off. Especially since Luc has also saved my life a few times since I've been here.

Anyway, back to my story. As I left *La Fleurette* that

gorgeous fall day to fill *les soeurs'* shopping list I had hopes of seeing Luc while I was in the village. I knew he had to go to Nice the next day and would miss tomorrow's harvest *fête* but I was hoping to see if he could come by the house for dinner tonight.

Without phones, emails or working fax machines, pretty much my only option to communicate with Luc was to go and knock on his door. I have no idea how single women did this sort of thing in the eighteen hundreds before smart phones were invented. Take it from me: it's absolutely impossible to play hard-to-get or have any mystery at all in post-apocalyptic France.

The village police *municipale* is located in the center of the village on the *place de la Maire*, named for the city hall which is also on the square. Bizarrely, the police station is one of the most beautiful buildings in the whole village. It's a two-story golden limestone building with terra cotta roof tiles and dark green shutters. Its double entrance doors, over a hundred years old, are a glossy ebony and features a French flag hanging over the entrance.

As I rode into the center of the village I spotted my friend Katrine Pelletier. A slim, attractive woman in her early forties, Katrine was standing next to a short bald man on the village square across from the village's WWI memorial.

I'd heard that Katrine was dating someone who was new to the village but I hadn't laid eyes on him yet because—and this seriously pains me to say—Katrine and I had a falling out a few months back which she has steadily resisted any and all attempts on my part to repair.

I'd like to say that the reason for her resistance was petty but the truth is, I'd let her down badly when she needed me and I couldn't blame her if she wanted to take her own sweet time in forgiving me.

I waved to her as I rode into town. She frowned and turned her back to continue talking to her new boyfriend.

That's okay, I thought, my cheeks burning. *I'll just keep trying. Every time she snubs me I'm sure she hates me a little less.*

Doesn't mean it doesn't hurt.

I dismounted in front of the police station and tied Roulette up to a wooden bar that had been erected out front. There were a couple of other horses tied up there too and for a second I got a flash of an Old West scene with all of us tying up our horses outside the saloon. Admittedly the goat that was also tied there sort of scrambled that image, but still.

Across from the police station was the village café. There weren't many people in the café this morning but one person you couldn't help but see was Theo Bardot, the owner of the café and the new mayor of Chabanel.

Theo was an odd bird in a lot of ways but as I watched him now braying with laughter with two pals sitting with him at the café, I couldn't help but think the most prominent evidence of his oddness had to be how hard he'd worked to become mayor—and how little he seemed to care about actually *being* mayor.

Even at forty yards, I could see he was wasted and it wasn't yet ten in the morning.

Marco, my husband and personal pet (as *les soeurs* often refer to him) was the sole waiter on duty this morning but even with fewer customers than usual, he looked busy. Of Mediterranean descent, Marco has olive skin complexion, dark brown eyes and silky dark hair. That description doesn't do justice to the fact that by anyone's estimation the man is seriously gorgeous.

I lifted a hand to wave to him but he was too swamped to notice me. I turned to the police station, my heart beating faster in anticipation of seeing Luc.

Katrine cuddled into Jean-Joseph's embrace as they walked away from the center of the village but she allowed herself a quick glance over her shoulder and watched Jules climb the stairs of the police station.

A part of her hated being so mean to Jules. The fact was she missed Jules. How could she not? They had been the closest of friends for nearly four years. It was Jules who had heard every thought, every worry, every fear that Katrine had felt for the whole of that time.

Life without Jules was like walking the dessert with no water—one painful, exhausting step at a time.

Katrine knew she could make it all go away—all the empty evenings without Jules, all the lost moments of shared laughter. All she had to do was forgive her. That's all.

But she couldn't.

Jules had shown herself to be no better than Katrine's ex-husband Gaultier. Faithless. Self-serving. Indifferent.

Jean-Joseph stopped and turned her around in his arms.

"You're upset," he said, his eyes narrowing at the expression on her face.

"No," she said.

She smiled up into his face and he kissed her. The blast of garlic and onions on his breath nearly froze the smile off her face but she squeezed her eyes shut and stayed steady.

She was lucky to have Jean-Joseph. In fact it was a miracle that she had him. Some nights she still couldn't believe that he would choose to be with *her* over anyone else in the village.

"Don't let the American ruin your morning," he scolded her as if reading her pained reaction to his kiss as her reaction to Jules.

"I'm not," she said, kissing him readily and at length. And realizing only later that she'd held her breath when she did.

3

DETAILS, DETAILS

Sergeant Eloise Basile leaned over Madame Gabin's desk at the police *municipale* and examined her work schedule over the receptionist's shoulder. The Chief had her and Detective Lieutenant Matteo working back to back again with a small overlap.

Eloise pressed her lips together and felt a tightening in her chest.

She knew she couldn't complain. With Romeo, their semi-retired part-timer now completely retired, it had to be this way.

Didn't leave much time for a social life, she thought with annoyance.

"I can make you a copy, Eloise," Madame Gabin said with unconcealed annoyance at having her private space impinged by Eloise's hovering.

"No, thanks. I can see I'm on duty around the clock."

"Then you are reading the schedule incorrectly since that is not how the Chief has assigned you at all."

Eloise sighed and straightened up.

It might as well be around the clock since these days Marco was always finding excuses for why we can't get together.

Just as Eloise was digesting these less than cheery thoughts, a motion outside one of the front floor to ceiling windows snagged her attention and she saw Jules Hooker tying her horse outside the police station.

A needle of annoyance stabbed her.

Lately, no excuse was greater than Marco needing to stay home and work.

He hadn't needed to "stay home and work" for the first five months she'd known him. It had only been once he'd been forced to marry the American to keep her safe from Grighot, the nearby alien detention camp, that somehow the work level had risen at *La Fleurette*, the farm house he shared with the American and two ninety-five year old twins.

"Is that all, Eloise?" Madame Gabin said testily. "I have work to do."

Eloise narrowed her eyes at the front door and waited for Jules to come through the door.

What nerve the woman had! First she tricked me into doing her a favor—one she knew could cost me my job!—and then she promised to give Marco an annulment when all along she never intended to.

Fury seethed in Eloise's gut as the door swung open and the object of her loathing stepped across the threshold.

"*Bonjour*, Eloise," Jules said, smiling broadly as if there was nothing at all wrong between them. "How are you this morning?"

It took all of Eloise's self-control not to spit in her face. That Jules could have wronged her so badly and then have the gall to come in and pretend they were still friends was unbelievable.

Had they *ever* been friends?

Forcing herself not to react, Eloise turned on her heel and walked out of the waiting room and back to her office.

Some day.

Some day I will get back what she took from me. From the Chief's good regard to Marco's love and my own self-respect.

I swear on all that is holy.

Some day.

"She still hates me," I said to Madame Gabin as I watched Eloise's retreating back.

"Can you blame her?"

I turned to look at the older woman but the way she narrowed her eyes at me reminded me of how *les soeurs* look at me when they're not in the mood to hear some obvious and totally expected prevarication of mine.

I guess when you get to a certain age, you just don't have time for all the bullshit.

"I told her I was sorry," I said.

"She probably knows you don't mean it."

Old people just don't pull their punches, you know?

"So you're saying I shouldn't expect Eloise to forgive me? Ever?"

The receptionist made a face. "I have lived long enough to know that sometimes the impossible is in fact quite possible."

So that was complete nonsense but I wisely refrained from rolling my eyes.

"Just today," Madame Gavin said, "I heard that old Madame Remay, easily fifty if she is a day is with child."

I gasped on cue.

"A surprise, no? And also to her husband who swears they have not had relations in two years."

"Oh, snap."

"And now the impossible has become all too possible for her and *le* Monsieur."

"So you're saying a fifty-year-old woman stands a better chance of getting pregnant than I do of Eloise forgiving me?"

"What can I help you with today?" Madame Gabin said sighing heavily and turning back to whatever excuse she uses for looking busy.

"Is Luc in?"

I craned my neck to glance down the hall. Now that I thought about it I hadn't seen his car out front.

Aside from my friend Thibault, Luc drives the only working car within fifty miles. It's an old clunker—*vintage* they used to call it—which explains why it wasn't affected by the EMP—something about its wires weren't electronic. I don't know all the science-y reasons why his car works when all the other newer cars stopped. I just know it runs and it's really uncomfortable to ride in.

"He is not," Madame Gabin said.

"Do you expect him back any time soon?" I asked sweetly.

"He will return when he does."

"Funny how that always happens. Should I wait?"

"That is up to you."

You're not going to believe me when I tell you that there was a time when Madame Gabin didn't like me.

I know she acts like I'm a major pain in her *derriere* but after Luc married the village drug addict a few months back —*long story*—Madame Gabin and my relationship took a huge step forward. It might sound like she was dismissing me just now and, okay, I'm pretty sure she *was* dismissing me, but I haven't lived in a small village for four years without learning *something* about people and how they think.

And one thing I know about Madame Gabin is that she likes to gossip.

"I passed Mayor Bardot on the way here," I said innocently. "He looked totally snockered."

Her eyes lit up. "It is true," she said eagerly. "Earlier and earlier, too. Disgraceful."

"Well, at least he's put together an amazing *fête* for tomorrow."

I knew for a fact that Theo had done bugger-all to put this harvest party on. If anything, Adrien Matteo—Luc's second in command—and Theo's secretary Madame LaTour had done all the work to make it happen.

And I knew Madame Gabin knew that very well.

"*Mais non!*" she said, shaking her head. "Monsieur Bardot has done nothing for the fête. *Rien!* Ever since he was elected, he has behaved as if he did not want to be mayor after all!"

Les soeurs and I had sat around the kitchen table on many nights since the election wondering about exactly this. Why was Theo behaving as if he never wanted to be mayor in the first place?

"I see Madame Pelletier has a new boyfriend," I said.

Madame Gabin actually scooted her chair closer to where I stood.

"Yes, *but*," she said meaningfully. "Does anyone know anything about him? He came to Chabanel two weeks ago looking for work but what kind of work does he do? Oh, he says he is happy to do physical labor but have you seen his hands? As soft as a baby's bottom! Something is going on with him, mark what I say."

Before I had a chance to ask her in a little more depth about what she knew of Eloise and her possible grudge match against *moi* the front door swung open and a middle-aged man whom I recognized as the village shoe and leather repair guy stood there panting.

"I need the police!" he said to Madame Gabin, his face red and glistening with sweat. "Someone has stolen my best goat!"

I swear I thought he was joking at first but Madame Gabin jumped to her feet and stood in the doorway to bellow down the hallway for either Eloise or Matteo to come quickly.

As she turned back to the poor agitated man, I sighed with the clear recognition that my opportunity to find out any more facts or gossip had closed for the foreseeable future.

I turned away to go do the twins' shopping.

Theo watched Katrine from where he sat at the café. He'd seen her with him before of course. Ever since the man arrived in the village he and Katrine could be seen walking together.

And worse.

Theo watched them now as Katrine brazenly lifted up on tiptoe to kiss the man on the mouth.

For a moment Theo thought he might be physically sick. The sky above seemed to swirl threateningly as if another EMP was about to strike. He gripped the edges of the table to attempt to keep his world from careening out of control.

Damn her! Damn her and her whorish behavior!

If not for her, if not for what she'd done, none of this would have happened to him.

Suddenly the light of the sky seemed to darken and Theo felt the alcohol and his own agitation sap his energy. His head sagged to his chest and then to his folded arms on the table.

And then to blessed oblivion.

4
THAT WHICH DOESN'T KILL YOU

The rest of my morning's errands didn't take long. I hit the *boulangerie* for the *brioche* and *pain au chocolat* the twins wanted, although why they wanted them I have no idea. The two of them bake up a storm on a daily basis but somehow there's always something for me to pick up at the bakery in the village.

Justine Becque and Léa Cazaly are an odd couple, especially for being twin sisters. Justine is a dear-heart and exactly who you'd imagine the quintessential Norman Rockwell style sweet old grandma might be.

Her twin Léa on the other hand is prickly, canny, impossible to predict and has a heart as deep as the Grand Canyon.

The two of them grow most of our produce in our back garden and cook better than any two Michelin chefs, I kid you not. I didn't know what delicious food was before I got trapped in post-apocalyptic France and moved in with them.

Justine was married at one point a thousand years ago but never had children and when she was widowed she and Léa, both veterans of the French Resistance during the last world war, threw in together. How I entered the picture is a tad more complicated but all I can say is, it works for all three of us.

I also needed to swing by the grocers because Léa had run out of chocolate and chocolate is one of the few things she can't make herself. I don't know where the grocer Monsieur Segal gets his chocolate since he probably doesn't have a patch of cacao beans growing in his back yard but since the black market is still frowned upon if not considered downright illegal I don't ask questions.

As I rode past the village square on my way out of town I saw that the café was less busy. Marco spotted me from where he stood, his hands on his hips, listening to a drinks order from one of the customers. He lifted a hand to wave. Theo was still sitting at one of the tables, now alone, with his head on his arms and snoring loudly.

I really did wonder what had happened to him. The transformation had been so quick. One moment he was a slightly obnoxious café owner running for mayor and the next, *boom!* he was the town drunk.

I scanned the square but still didn't see evidence of Luc's car so there was no point in stopping back in at the police *municipale*. I didn't see Katrine or her new boyfriend either. I sighed and pressed my heels into Roulette's flank.

I still think what I did to Katrine was completely forgivable—understandable even. But of course it wasn't me who needed to forgive. I honestly would have expected Katrine to relent before now.

Maybe I'd misjudged her. Maybe she really was through with me for good.

I held these less than perky thoughts throbbing in my brain as I maneuvered Roulette out of the village at a walk.

It was a cool, sunny day and that was a classic recipe for Roulette to try something diabolical.

I don't know what his life was like as a plow horse with his owner Monsieur Dellaux, but with me he always seemed to be either trying to unseat me and run back to his stall and dinner bucket, or...no, that was pretty much his only goal.

At least now he would usually run back to *La Fleurette* after he threw me. The first couple of weeks I had him he'd take off and head for whichever farmer's field was closest and full of the tastiest clover. Now at least he knew his food bucket lived at *La Fleurette* and so that's where he went.

La Fleurette is a little over two miles outside Chabanel and once I'd broken free of the village and its cobblestone streets, I kept a tighter rein on Roulette. This was when he tended to see blue skies ahead and often took it into his head to race back to the old food bucket at top speed. There was a pasture off the main road that nobody used anymore and from there it was more or less a straight shot to my house.

I closed my legs around Roulette and sank my seat bones deep into the saddle. On a normal horse, this would've told him in no uncertain terms to stop moving but on Roulette it just kept him at a nice steady walk. With two saddlebags full of chocolate bars and some of Madame Roullion's homemade *tapenade*—the latter in three glass containers—I didn't want to take the chance of him bolting.

We hadn't gone a half a mile outside the village when I felt Roulette quiver beneath me. Like I said, this horse will shy at a butterfly sneeze so I shortened up his reins.

"Whoa. Don't even *think* about it," I said, keeping my voice level.

Roulette tossed his head and I had a brief image of him taking off, ejecting me with great flying arcs of baked goods, chocolate and black olive paste in the process, when suddenly the object of Roulette's concern revealed himself.

Not unlike a lot of people, a horse is more fearful of what he *thinks* he sees than what he actually sees. Hearing movement on the perimeter of the little forest where we were riding was much more terrifying to Roulette than seeing a six-foot man emerge from its inky shadows.

I mean, he still wasn't happy, but I could tell he wasn't on the verge of bolting at least.

The man must have spotted us riding across the pasture because he waved and began limping toward us.

Roulette pawed impatiently at the ground as I watched the man approach. I don't want you to think I'm foolhardy. I more than most people know how evil people can be these days—especially strangers—but because I was on horseback and because I didn't see any weapons on the guy I felt pretty confident. Plus, unless he was faking it, he looked injured.

I let him get within twenty yards.

"Excuse me, Monsieur," I said. "Stop there, please."

The man stopped and grinned. This was the point that I noted that he was good-looking in a rugged sort of way. That meant he had a few scars on him that I could see and when he smiled there was a tooth missing. But with his mouth shut, and his curly brown hair and broad shoulders, he was handsome.

"You are English?" he asked, squinting up at me through the sun. He was wearing a jacket but it looked too small for him. Had he stolen it? Gotten too fat for it?

"None of your beeswax," I said, wondering where the hell I'd heard that expression. "What are you doing here?"

"I twisted my ankle in the woods. Can you help me, Mademoiselle?"

I have to tell you I think I'm a pretty good judge of character. Now granted there have been a few times when I've been way off but I'm relatively sure those were exceptions to the rule.

The way I read this situation was that this poor guy needed my help and if I've learned anything during the last four years it is that we can all use a helping hand from time to time.

I swung down from the saddle.

5

ONCE BURNED

Luc parked his car outside the police station. As soon as he got out of the car he noticed Marco Alaoui waiting tables at the Sucre Café.

To be perfectly honest Luc didn't just *happen* to notice Marco since he was pretty much always aware of him. How could he not be?

Luc was in love with the man's wife.

The fact was, Jules Hooker did things to Luc's insides that no sane man should endure and yet Luc loved every miserable, exquisite moment with her. He'd registered her effect on him from the beginning, from the very instant he'd laid eyes on her. Regardless of how he'd tried to keep her at arms' length—for *years*—he was in love and he knew it.

Luc turned his attention from the café and grabbed his briefcase from the back seat of the car before heading into the police *municipale*. He of all people knew that Jules and Marco's marriage, although legal, wasn't real.

But still, it rankled. Especially when Luc thought of how close *he* himself had come to being the one to rescue Jules from the prospect of incarceration at Grighot, where all non-nationals had been herded in the wake of the EMP.

No, Luc knew he should be grateful to Marco.

And perhaps he would've been if the man had been just a little less handsome. There wasn't a woman in the village under sixty who wasn't in love with Marco Alaoui

Luc swung open the front door and nodded at Madame Gabin whose face brightened at the sight of him.

"*Bonjour*, Chief DeBray. Are you here long?"

Luc parked his briefcase on her desk and picked up his messages.

"Unfortunately no. Are Matteo and Eloise in?"

Luc hated to miss the festival tomorrow—not least because he'd have liked to have gone to it with Jules—but he needed to make sure Matteo and Eloise were comfortable with what to expect tomorrow. While Luc had every confidence in them Eloise had been acting a little temperamental lately.

"Only Detective Matteo, Chief. Eloise was feeling under the weather but said she'd be back for her rounds this evening."

Luc grunted but before he could head down the hall to speak with Matteo, Madame Gabin stopped him.

"Madame Hooker was here looking for you."

Luc glanced at his watch but realized what he already knew: he didn't have time to swing by *La Fleurette*. As it was he was going to miss the first hour of the crime symposium in Nice, something he was sure his superior officer Michel Lestrange would be sure to notice.

"Tell Eloise to run by *La Fleurette* when she does her rounds and let Jules and *les soeurs* know I had to leave early and I'll see them when I return."

"Yes, Chief. I'll tell Eloise of course."

If there was any hint of irony in her voice—or any lack of confidence that Eloise would in fact deliver Luc's message as he'd intended—Luc was unaware of it.

Marie Dionne stood trembling at the door of her shack, her naked body covered only by filthy rags and a cheap voile netting she'd stolen off a corpse in the churchyard one night years ago.

She dug her nails into the palms of her hand to quell the quivering she felt in her limbs as she revisited the meeting with *him* in her mind.

Never in a million years had she expected him to find her! Especially not after the EMP had obliterated all modes of communication.

How had he found her?

She turned to pick up the burning cigarette from the ashtray and her hand froze, as usual her eyes struck by the scarred and damaged protuberance at the end of her arm. She felt transfixed as she stared at it, her anger and fear merging to form a cataclysmic mushroom cloud of fury.

How could she be shocked that he would try to find her?

Her only real surprise was that she hadn't had the wit and presence of mind to kill him outright.

Next time, he wouldn't catch her off guard.

Next time, she would be ready.

6

STICK A FORK IN IT

I have to say the twins were not pleased.

Because the injured man—his name was René Deroy—had a sprained ankle I'd had to put him on Roulette and walk back to *La Fleurette*. By the time Deroy slid down to the ground in the front drive of our *mas*, I had blisters on my heels and had been nearly stepped on twice by my own stupid horse.

Using their built-in radar for potential trouble, both Justine and Léa came out of the house as Deroy hobbled over to the rattan bench on the front porch and sat down.

"Who is this?" Léa asked sharply, her hands on her hips, her eyes drilling into the poor man.

Justine was right behind her and was likewise not thrilled with what I had dragged home.

My dog Cocoa bolted out the front door behind them, her tongue lolling, her tail wagging, right up until she saw the newcomer. Then I saw her hackles go up and her head lower. Even from where I was standing twenty-five feet away, I could hear the growl deep in her throat.

"Cocoa, stop that," I said, snapping my fingers at the dog

which sent her running to me to stand by my knees while still glowering at the stranger.

"He's hurt," I said to the twins. I pulled the saddlebags off Roulette, careful to keep a hand on his reins so he wouldn't head back to his stall without me. I passed both bags to Justine.

"Who are you?" Léa asked René. "How are you hurt?"

"It is my ankle," René said, trying to smile. Even I could see he was in pain and he was exhausted. It hadn't been possible to converse with him on the horse and me leading so I still knew almost nothing about him.

Léa turned to me with the same look she'd given René. Her words were short and clipped.

"He can sleep in the barn," she said and then turned on her heel, signaling for Cocoa to come with her.

Now, we live in a massive *mas* which is a kind of farmhouse from the middle ages.

In case I haven't mentioned it, *La Fleurette* is a twelfth-century carriage house situated on a small rise surrounded by fields and bordered on one side by a country road which separates us from a large copse of trees.

The back garden is encased by an ancient stonewall that the cats—we have three—are always leaping off of like it's some great adventure to explore the other side. There's a decrepit terrace off the back of the house with more broken pavers than flat stones and a *potager* that is Léa's own private domain and where we get most of our daily veggies and herbs.

The point I'm laboring to make is that we have no fewer than *seven* bedrooms and five of those are outfitted with beds and linens. In other words, there is no reason for this poor man to sleep on hay in the freezing barn tonight.

"Look," I said to him. "I'll talk to her."

But he waved away my words. "The barn will be fine," he said. "The best I've had in months."

I had to get Roulette untacked, brushed and fed but I very much wanted to continue this conversation with Monsieur Deroy.

I understand that in the summer months people down on their luck are forced to sleep in fields and ditches but *what* had driven him to do it? Did he not have any people? Where was his village? What had he been doing before the lights went out?

But Roulette swung his head around, narrowly missing my forehead so I knew my questions would have to wait.

That night the twins were busy with last-minute preparations for the harvest festival. They were making multiple *pissaladiers* which is a dish I happen to love and they don't make it nearly enough for me. A *pissaladier* is a kind of pizza only way better and chocked full of olives and even sardines. A trial one had been made for our dinner tonight.

My mouth watered at the thought of it.

After I'd fed Roulette and led him into the paddock to graze, I went back for René where he sat at the front of the house. He limped along beside me as I showed him the outdoor well where he could clean up. An hour later I gave him a blanket and brought him a plate of food since both Justine and Léa were adamant they didn't want him in the house.

I was shocked at their reaction to René. These are two of the most generous, charitable people I know. There was obviously something about René they didn't like and either they couldn't put their finger on what it was or they didn't want to say. But bottom line, they were not having him in the house.

"Tell him he's to be gone in the morning," Léa said.

"I told him," I said. "He's injured, you know."

"It is only a sprain," Justine said.

If you could know how astonishing it was to hear soft-hearted Justine Becque discount a man's injuries you'd be as shocked as I was. Mind you, like I said, Justine and Léa lived through the Nazi occupation and witnessed some serious grade-A atrocities during that time. They had a sixth sense about people that I've long come to respect it. Usually.

As I walked down the garden path to deliver the plate of food to René I realized that I wouldn't blame the sisters for disparaging a sprained ankle in an otherwise healthy male. In fact—and I was seriously annoyed with them for putting the thought in my head—now that they'd set me down this mental trajectory, I couldn't help but think it was pretty wimpy of René to be lounging about the forest and then to happily agree to take my place on my horse.

I couldn't imagine Luc behaving like that. Not unless he was missing a leg.

And maybe not even then.

Granted, using Luc as any kind of measuring stick for other men was not fair since he's incredibly brave and wonderful.

But still. Come on. A sprained ankle?

Thinking of Luc reminded me that he wouldn't be at the *fête* tomorrow. I hated that. I also hated missing seeing him today. We'd only officially become an item six weeks ago.

All of our previous misfires, and trust me there have been a few of them, were either behind us or only served to remind us of how much we'd been through together and bonded us even closer.

Like many men, Luc is taciturn which means I do most of the talking. Sometimes that bugs me because it feels like I'm the only one defining the relationship and he's just agreeing or worse, choosing not to weigh-in so as to keep things light. My past experiences of trying to force him to commit to an opinion has generally not ended well.

Like I said, this is one instance where Luc is not that different from most guys I've known. But it's a pretty small thing to overcome for all the other amazing benefits he brings to the table.

Wow. Really sounds like I'm negotiating a real estate deal, doesn't it?

When I reached the shed behind the garden and handed René a plate of *ratatouille* and *pissaladier*, he broke into a big grin and quickly began to devour the contents using his fingers. I wondered if it had been very long since his last good meal or if he was just a pig.

"So how come you were in the forest?" I asked.

He glanced up at me, his cheeks bulging with food. "Short cut," he said.

That made sense.

"Short cut to where?"

He swallowed with difficulty and reached for the half baguette I'd tucked under my arm.

"Chabanel."

"Oh, so you know Chabanel?"

He nodded. "Been there once before."

"Do you know anyone there?"

His eyes glittered for a moment at the question but whatever I thought I saw in them was quickly gone. "*Oui.* A friend or two."

"Who are they? Maybe I know them."

Instead of answering me, he waved his hand at me apologetically. "Do you mind if I rest now? My foot is quite painful."

"Yeah, sure. No problem." I turned in the open archway of the shed and glanced around. Granted it wasn't the Ritz but it would keep him dry tonight if it rained and it would protect him from the cold October night air. I needn't feel bad about not having him sleep in the house.

As if that was even an option with the twins.

"Okay, well, Monsieur Deroy, sleep well. You'll need to leave first thing in the morning."

"Of course. Good night, Mademoiselle."

I headed back to the house but something buzzed around the edges of my memory. Remember how I said I'm a good judge of character? Well, naturally I also know now how this little piece of my story plays out and it's possible that right about now—with Deroy's obvious hesitancy to tell me why he was in the area—I was starting to think that maybe I was wrong about René being a good guy.

Okay, okay. So as it turned out I was totally wrong about him. I know now that the guy was a complete scoundrel and thank God the twins didn't allow him into the house overnight. But I didn't know that at the time.

So, back to my story...

When I came back to the house our neighbor Monsieur Moutier was sitting in the kitchen drinking a cup of coffee with Léa and Justine.

"Monsieur Moutier has come with a message for us," Léa said.

"Oh?" I sat down with them but didn't pour myself any coffee. It was nearly ten at night. Don't ask me how it is everyone in France is able to drink espresso this late without being wide awake all night but somehow they do.

Cocoa was in one of her many dog beds under the table but her eyes were watching me.

"Monsieur Moutier says that Marco sent him a message for us that he will stay the night in Chabanel tonight," Justine said.

"Really?"

That surprised me because although Marco often spent the night in Chabanel at Eloise's place I knew he was trying to break up with her. In fact I'm sure I remembered he said today was the day he was going to tell her for sure.

I think it's important to mention here that Marco wasn't just some stray that I'd picked up along the way. He'd been with me on an ill-fated sail out of Marseille last spring when the boat owner was murdered and the crime laid at his feet by the victim's wife and murderer.

With my friend Thibault's help, I was able to get Marco out of Marseille and I'd spent the last six months trying to think of a way to prove his innocence and bring the real murderer to justice.

So far, my efforts had amounted to a lot of thinking and no real action.

I glanced at Léa's face and saw she was glaring at me.

You know how when you live with someone you can decipher their moods with just a glance?

Léa had been counting on Marco coming home tonight because she didn't like having a stranger in the barn.

I also knew that both she and Justine were in possession of ancient WWII rifles and that Léa at least would be sleeping with hers on the floor by her bed.

∼

My guess was that it was either the middle of the night or some time in the early morning when I heard Cocoa's frenetic barking. She usually sleeps with me so hearing her barking from another part of the house had me out of the bed and down the slick stone stairs before I was even fully awake.

I made it to the foyer, the frigid slabs of centuries-old stone beneath my naked feet drilling numbing cold up my legs, where I saw two shadowy figures in our front salon.

One I recognized without any trouble. Léa stood in her nightgown between me and the other figure. In front of her I could hear Cocoa, her barking having given way to threatening growls.

"What's going on?" I shouted, my voice more a croak than anything that might frighten an intruder.

"Ask your friend," Léa said as she cocked the rifle she held to her shoulder.

I sidestepped Léa just as Justine appeared from behind me with a lantern. The light illuminated the scene of René Deroy standing in the salon facing us, one hand holding a bulging sack.

7

SON OF A GUN

Katrine sat up in bed. The sounds of the night had crept through her bedroom window but truthfully, that wasn't what had awakened her. She glanced at the alarm clock on her bedside table. Three o'clock. She hadn't slept a moment since she'd gone to bed. Her head was buzzing with too many muddled hopes, unhappy thoughts and tortured memories.

She swung her legs out of bed and reached for her robe, slipping on her slippers as she made her way across the room.

She'd been lucky to move in with her mother when Gaultier had gone away. Her mother had taken over this apartment—one she'd always coveted—when the owners left to live with relations in Lyons after the EMP.

Three bedrooms. Unheard of in a village the size of Chabanel. But it meant Suzanne and Katrine each had their own room while Katrine's two daughters Annette and Babette shared a room.

I should be grateful, Katrine thought as she moved down

the hall to her daughters' room and peeked inside. They slept peacefully.

Why am I not grateful? Why am I sick with self-loathing and resentment for how things ended up for me?

No husband, no money, no income, no house of her own.

And the one friend she'd have given anything for, done anything for—betrayed her at the first opportunity.

As had Gaultier.

Is it something about me?

Katrine moved into the kitchen. It was a full moon tonight and the kitchen was illuminated through a small window over the sink.

She lit the gas lighter on the stove and watched the blue flame jump to form a wobbly circle. She put the kettle on the ring of fire and brought down a stoneware mug and dropped a chamomile teabag into it. Then she went to the kitchen table to sit and wait.

Wait for the water to boil, wait for the dawn, wait for my life to be over.

"I thought I heard a noise in here," her mother said loudly as she came into the kitchen squinting in the dim room, a lighted candle held in one hand.

"I'm sorry if I woke you," Katrine said, feeling an ominous prickling on her scalp.

Dear God, do I not even get a moment in the middle of the night away from her?

"Those teabags cost money, you know. And you aren't bringing any in. You do know I'm feeding your children, yes?"

You mean, your grandchildren? Katrine wanted to say.

"Yes, Mother. I'm sorry. I'll remind them to eat less."

"I do not appreciate your sarcasm!" Suzanne said

sharply, her voice threatening to wake the girls. "How dare you speak to me like that!"

"I'm sorry, Mother," Katrine said, getting up to pour the boiling water into her cup and for one wild moment imagining throwing it at her mother where she stood in the kitchen.

"You're not sorry. You're a taker just like your father. Just like your useless excuse of a husband!"

"I know. I'm sorry, Mother." Katrine felt a hollowness settle in her chest.

"If you had any sense at all you'd get Jean-Joseph to marry you tomorrow—before he hears the gossip around the village about who you really are. He's your only chance, Katrine. There won't be too many more stooges coming into town willing to have you!"

Katrine nodded, her eyes riveted on the mug of steaming tea she gripped tightly in her hands.

I should be grateful I should be grateful I should be grateful

8
ONE FOR THE ROAD

Deroy looked from Léa's face to mine as if trying to gauge which one would be the bigger patsy for his line of crap. His eyes rested on me.

I don't know whether it was the pain of realizing this guy had taken advantage of my good nature or the fact that I'd now never hear the end of it from Léa but I was seconds from giving Cocoa the green light to take this guy's adenoids out.

"Mademoiselle, *please*," he said in a wheedling tone.

"Put the bag down," I said. "I'm totally cool with her shooting you so don't test me."

He dropped the bag which made a loud clanking sound —like dishes or silver candlesticks might make when dropped on a hard floor. The sound served to trigger me into a barely contained rage.

"Get out," I said. "Put your hands in the air and get the hell out."

"Please, Mademoiselle. I will go back to the barn and—"

"On the count of three. Be gone or she shoots you. One—"

"I go! I go!" he said as he moved to the front door. "But this is an outrage! You won't even listen to my perfectly reasonable—"

"Two...!"

"I am leaving!" He wrenched open the front door and stumbled out into the night. Honestly, he didn't look like he was limping at all.

Yep, I'm a patsy. A big king-sized idiot patsy.

"You will be sorry for this!" he shouted over his shoulder as he moved across the driveway.

"I think I will shoot him anyway," Léa said.

"Well, you know best," I said, not at all sure she wasn't serious.

"Now, now, Léa," Justine said soothingly. "He is leaving and we don't want to clean up the mess when we have such a full day tomorrow."

Wow. Justine is as crazy as her sister.

Cocoa chased Deroy out past the gravel drive where he turned and pulled back his leg as if to kick her.

"You do it and you're dead!" I shouted.

By the light of the moon I saw Deroy shake his fist at me instead and hurry away.

Nope, definitely not limping.

I called Cocoa back who gave him a few last-word barks that sounded very much like doggie French for *"And don't come back!"*

I turned to Léa who was lowering her rifle.

"You were right," I said.

She snorted which was her subtle way of saying *Of course.* Or maybe it meant *you're an idiot.* The sound is cultural and highly idiomatic so it could be either one.

Justine went to the dropped bag and pulled out two

silver candlesticks badly in need of polishing and the *brioche* I'd bought that morning at the *boulangerie*.

"The bastard!" Léa growled when she saw the *brioche*. Like most French people, things didn't start getting serious until you messed with her food.

"I promise," I said to both of them as I ruffled the ears on my happy warrior dog. "No more bringing in strays of the two-legged variety. Which reminds me, where's Twig?"

Twig was Marco's over-excited half-breed boxer puppy who was way more trouble than he was worth. It was unlike Twig to have slept through tonight's activities.

"Marco gave him to Sergeant Basile," Justine said solemnly. "As a gift."

"Some gift." I couldn't imagine what Marco was up to, giving Twig to Eloise. The only thing I could imagine was that Eloise, thinking to ingratiate herself with *les soeurs,* had offered to take the dog off their hands and Marco—wanting to be shed of Eloise—agreed to it in hopes that it would make her hate him less when he dumped her.

"I'm sorry about all this," I said.

Léa raised the bolt handle on the rifle to block the firing mechanism and went to shut the front door but it was Justine who spoke.

"You will never go wrong erring on the side of kindness to your fellow man," Justine said solemnly.

I looked at her in surprise.

"Really? Thanks, Justine. That means a lot to—"

And then Léa and she both burst out laughing and Justine gave my arm an affectionate squeeze as she and Léa turned to make their way back upstairs to bed.

Have I mentioned how much I love these two?

9
TAKE ME TO THE FAIR

The next morning, we were all up early to get ready for the harvest festival. I had to feed the animals—a horse, a dog, three cats, four goats and a dozen chickens—get the stove fire going long enough for the three of us to have a decent cup of coffee, and secure the garden toolshed.

Les soeurs were putting the finishing touches on their *pissaladiers* and jars of blackberry wine and loading everything up in the horse cart which was parked out front of our *mas*.

Cocoa accompanied me to the shed. I was pretty sure Deroy hadn't tried to come back and sleep in the shed because Cocoa would've known and notified us but I was a little worried that Deroy might have damaged the shed in some way before leaving.

I found Roulette with his head hanging over the paddock fence waiting for his breakfast so I quickly put together his grains in a bucket and hooked it where he could eat it without having to move him. Then I checked the shed and found the blanket I'd given Deroy and also the empty dish from the dinner I'd brought him.

What I *didn't* find were the two hoof picks, a curry brush and my favorite green-handled utility knife that I kept on the shelf on the far wall.

I ground my teeth and felt a vein pulsing over my right eye.

"Try to be nice to someone and just see where it gets you," I grumbled under my breath to Cocoa. It still amazed me that the man had taken advantage of my hospitality so badly. He'd allowed us to feed and shelter him and then had the nerve to steal from us!

Cocoa sniffed the ground where Deroy had lain but I didn't see any other evidence that the man had been there. Roulette inhaled his breakfast and I quickly brushed him down, cleaned out his feet with a long nail I found, and with Cocoa at my heels led him to the front of the house to hook him up to the cart.

I wisely decided not to mention the tools theft to the twins since they already had enough ammunition to support their belief that I was a total chump.

It took us an hour to finish packing the cart and another hour to make our way around Chabanel to where the festival was being held in the adjoining field. Because of the cart, we needed to stay on a paved road as much as possible which gave us fewer options for routes. But the weather was cool and the sun was already out so nobody minded the longer ride.

Cocoa sat up front with Léa—who was driving the cart —and Justine who held a pot of her famous *cassoulet* on her knees as if it were a casserole lined in gold.

From the back of the cart I listened to the birds singing in the overhead trees as we rode along and let my mind wander. It's a lot of work keeping our house and grounds producing food for us. Just to get the stove going in the morning I have to cut about thirty minutes worth of kindling. So any opportunity I have to just sit and watch the clouds scud by is one I grab with both hands and relish.

As we crested a small hill east of Chabanel I saw that people had set up tables along the rows of grape vines. A large metal spit had been erected on which hung a hog that one of the villagers had butchered the day before. Old Madame Ruset and her daughters were basting and seasoning the slowly rotating pork.

The heavenly aroma of the roasting meat seemed to surround us like a delightful fog as we approached and I couldn't help looking forward to the meal later when the meat would be falling off the spit in tender, juicy slabs.

I waved to Madame Gavin where she sat near the *charcuterie* table. She already held a glass of wine in her hand.

Léa stopped the cart at the end of a long line of tables. A couple of men were digging a pit of some kind that would probably be where we'd all hang out later this evening drinking and eating whatever food was left from the day. I wondered idly if the French knew how to make 'smores.

As I got out of the cart I saw that the table nearest us was loaded with baked goods—pies and cakes, cookies, beignets and baguettes. Another table near the rotating pork was covered with platters of roasted potatoes and crocks of *aïoli* —the Provencal garlic mayonnaise I've become addicted to —and plate after plate of grilled carrots, parsnips, broccoli and cauliflower.

Beyond the food tables some of the men had set up

competition sites for horseshoes, *boules*, and even a big rope for tug-of-war. A few people had guitars.

The area was plenty big enough for all the food tables and for people to sit on stools or blankets on the ground but the French love to dance at their parties and I honestly couldn't see how that was going to happen in a pasture. But then, where there's a will…

"Jules!"

I turned to see Marco running up to me from down a long row of grape vines, his eyes sparkling as usual. Marco may not be the sharpest blade in the toolbox but he was genuinely cheerful most of the time and that counts for a lot in life.

"Hey, Marco," I said as he reached me and we quickly greeted each other with kisses on both cheeks. "You look like you slept in your clothes."

"Long story," he said with a sigh. "But there is a man running around telling everyone that you threatened him with his life."

I felt a rush of adrenaline tingling through my chest at his words.

"Are you kidding me?" I said. "He tried to steal from us last night!"

"*Vraiment?*"

After I filled him in on the whole story, Marco's face darkened and I have to say it was a new look for him—one I'd never seen before. He's normally so jolly and chipper.

"If I had been there," he said earnestly, "I would have thrashed him within an inch of his life."

"Yeah, so why weren't you there? I thought you were trying to break up with Eloise not go for Round Two."

"I *am* trying to break up with her! But she is using her wiles on me."

"So you're saying she seduced you?"

"*Exactement!*"

"Wow, she really knows what strings to pull with you, doesn't she?"

But he looked so distraught over not being home when we needed him that I didn't have the heart to give him too much of a hard time.

"It doesn't matter," I said. "No harm done. So are you breaking up with her today?"

He nodded grimly. "It is killing me," he said. "She is a sweet girl and I am very fond of her—"

"Yeah, yeah," I said, moving to loosen the harness straps across Roulette's withers. "Help me unload, will you?" I could see Léa and Justine had already staked out one of the outdoor tables as their own.

As Marco unloaded the cart I found a good place to hobble Roulette where he could graze but not get into too much trouble. I couldn't help but scan the slowly growing crowd to see if I could spot Deroy.

If he was going around telling people that the problem was with *me*—and he was probably doing it to get *his* version of the story out first—I probably should talk to Detective Matteo and make a formal complaint about what really happened last night.

I spied Eloise in the crowd. I could see by the way her head swiveled and her eyes narrowed that she was looking for Marco.

Poor Marco. Today was definitely not going to be all fun and games for him.

10

BUSTING A MOVE

Marie clutched her cardigan tightly around her shoulders and wove her way through the dense vineyard on the way to the food tables and kiosks. She tried to ignore the looks she was getting from the villagers.

When she'd come up with this plan last night she hadn't totally discounted the fact that she would stick out. After all, in the eight years she'd lived on the edge of Chabanel, she'd never once gone into town herself, shopped at the bakery, had a drink at the café or exchanged a single greeting with anyone.

Even if she'd disguised herself as someone other than who she was, the mere fact that she was a stranger in the village would have been cause for raised eyebrows.

She knew that René would be here today. *Pass up a chance for free food and wine?* She couldn't imagine it.

The tenth time one of the villagers turned and glared at her in appalled disgust, Marie tucked her head and cursed her stupidity for thinking there would be enough strangers in the crowd that she wouldn't be noticed. She jammed both hands into her cardigan pocket, clutching her right hand tightly into a fist.

How did they know who she was? Was there something about her that just shouted *whore*?

She felt her chest constrict in self-loathing.

Very probably.

But it didn't matter.

She forced herself to keep walking, keeping to the edges of the vineyard rows and away from the tables where most people were congregating.

All she needed to do was find him, lure him deeper into the vineyard, some place far and quiet.

And finish this nightmare once and for all.

By midday, the roasting pork was done and everyone had settled into their places for the day. Since it was a vineyard there were no big plane trees to shade under but it was October so the sun was weak in any case.

Marco had scooted off seemingly to spend the bulk of his day avoiding Eloise. He'd revealed that his strategy was to catch her just before the *fête* was over, deliver the bad news, and then catch a ride back to *La Fleurette* with me and *les soeurs*. He assumed Eloise wouldn't dare create a scene any where near the Cazaly sisters.

Once I got the twins settled at their table, with Cocoa happily curled up underneath it, and all the food spread out for sharing with friends and neighbors, I went to explore the festival and to sample any delicacies from the other tables.

Old Monsieur Breten had somehow gotten a ride to Cassis this week and he'd come back with enough *boquerones,* which are anchovies in vinegar and oil, and sea urchins to sell to the market vendors as well as share at the festival. Personally I think sea urchins are an acquired taste and not wanting to interfere with anyone else's chance of enjoying them, I stuck to the oysters and sardines. It was nice getting a taste of brine in the middle of a vineyard. The food we eat at *La Fleurette* is fresh and pulled straight from the ground but there is a tinge of monotony to it that I know from years past will only get worse as we go into winter.

I saw Marco chowing down on some boiled shrimp and was reminded that he came from Marseille and probably missed seafood. I nearly laughed when I saw him catch a glimpse of Eloise, gulp down his glass of homemade beer and melt into the crowd.

When I spotted Eloise emerge from one of the vine rows, her face creased with a determined frown, my heart went out to Marco. She was definitely not going to make this easy on him.

On the other hand, I also felt a twinge of guilt for the lie I'd told last summer to get her to do me a favor. It was no wonder she was mad at me. But even *she* had to know that poor feckless Marco was trying in his dumb, sloppy way to end things with her.

A familiar laugh floated up above the crowd and I turned and caught a glimpse of Katrine standing not fifteen yards from me. She appeared to be talking to a woman whose face I couldn't immediately see. Katrine's new boyfriend Jean-Joseph was a few yards away having a glass of *pastis* with Monsieur Benet who ran the post office.

I pushed through the crowd toward Katrine.

"Hey, Katrine," I said breathlessly when I reached her. "Quite a crowd, huh?"

When I approached the woman Katrine was speaking

with snapped her head around to look at Katrine for her reaction so I guess our feud was officially legendary.

I know Katrine pretty well and I know she shies away from public displays of any kind. She might be fine with snubbing me in the marketplace but she'd be much less comfortable being rude to me in front of an audience.

Or at least I hoped so.

Katrine's face whitened when she saw me and her eyes darted around the crowd to find her boyfriend.

Katrine has a problem with men. Just one meeting with her ex-husband would tell you that. She looks to them for approval even if they're the biggest slime-ball on the planet.

Now, regardless of what old Madame Gabin said about Katrine's new boyfriend, I don't know anything about him. He might be perfectly nice.

Except that isn't the kind of man Katrine is drawn to.

But her desperate scanning of the crowd for him made it was clear she was already using him as a crutch, or in my case—a barrier to put between us.

"Excuse me, Janice," Katrine said to her companion, "I must check on the children."

"I can see the kids from here," I said cheerfully. "They're right over there playing in the grass."

Janice slunk off leaving the two of us.

"So I see you have a new beau," I said. "How did you meet him?"

"Why are you harassing me like this?" Katrine hissed.

"See there's that cultural divide again," I said. "In my country, asking someone how they're doing is considered a normal social interaction."

"I have made it clear that I want nothing to do with you."

"Which is your prerogative. But only after you've listened to my apology."

"I am not interested in your apology."

"Well, that's just silly. Surely you owe me that."

"Why do you think I owe you anything after what you did?" she said, her voice shrill.

"*Chérie?*" Jean-Joseph strode to her side and slipped an arm around her waist, his eyes glaring at me.

"*Bonjour*," I said, sticking my hand out. "I'm Jules."

Ignoring my hand, he drew Katrine closer to him.

"I know who you are," he sniffed. "Madame Pelletier is not interested in associating with you."

"You probably don't know that Katrine and I are on a first-name basis. Right, Katrine? Because of all that nearly-dying together stuff we lived through? Remember?"

"I remember you were responsible for putting my husband in prison," Katrine said primly, not looking at me.

"Okay, now I know you're joking. Gaultier tried to *strangle* you. Are you telling me you don't remember him with his pudgy little fingers wrapped around your throat?"

"Jean-Joseph," Katrine murmured into the chest of her protector, "please take me away from this."

"Good God, Katrine!" I said in exasperation. "If you don't want to be friends any more, fine!"

I could sense a small knot of very interested, noisy villagers were gathering around the three of us.

"But you don't need some guy to escort you back to your picnic table. Unless I was really wrong about you on just about every level."

"You will not speak to her like that!" Jean-Joseph said.

I took a step toward him until I was right in his face. "Or what?"

His face went purple with indecision. He took a step back, dragging Katrine with him. "*Incroyable!*"

The crowd laughed which of course made it all worse

and I could see Katrine was on the verge of humiliated tears. I hadn't meant for this to happen and yes, I know I say that a lot and yes, I can see I'd made it all worse.

I was seconds from retiring from the field when harsh shouts erupted just a few yards from us and the attention of our fickle audience shifted from us to whatever unexpected entertainment was going on over there.

I let the crowd push past me as the unmistakable sounds of fists hitting flesh and screaming oaths and shouts revealed what was clearly a physical altercation of some kind happening.

I didn't even care.

My eyes, stinging with tears that I was determined not to shed I turned away from the throng. I hated myself for making it worse and I was furious with Katrine for being so unforgiving and cruel. I stumbled away from the crowd, desperately needing to be alone for a few minutes.

Why is she being so hard-hearted? Why can't she understand that I had no choice but to do what I did?

I walked for only a few minutes until I stood on the verge of the vineyard. I wiped the tears from my face and took in several long breaths to steady my emotions.

From this vantage point the vineyard looked bleak and forlorn, its fruit stripped and leaves blowing haphazardly down the long irregular rows. The temperature seemed to have fallen too and I shivered inside my wool pullover and denim jacket.

In the distance I could hear guitars and fiddles had started up so whatever fight had erupted must have been settled somehow. I wondered if there was a first aid tent at the festival.

Just when I was about to turn back to check on the

twins, I heard the faint but unmistakable sounds of weeping.

Frowning, I walked to the end of the first grape row and looked down it. There, on her knees was a small girl. She was wearing a yellow and blue Disney Belle dress. I couldn't help but think that she hadn't been old enough to have seen the movie before the EMP went off.

"*Chérie?*" I called to her. "Are you lost?"

I wasn't sure how that was possible since the noise from the festival was quite loud.

She looked up at me, her eyes luminous with tears and her bottom lip quivered.

"*Mon petit chien*," she said.

"Your puppy?" I looked around. "You've lost your puppy?"

She nodded and I held a hand out to her.

I might not be able to patch things up with Katrine or get back into Eloise's good graces or fix Marco's problems—but one thing I could do was help a little girl find her puppy.

11

MONSTERS UNDER THE BED

Why does she keep at me? Katrine thought unhappily. *Why can't she just accept we're done?*

Because you're not, a little voice said in her head.

Katrine gripped Jean-Joseph's hand tightly which made him spill the wine he was holding.

Why is she putting both of us through this? I can't forgive what she's done. I just can't.

"You should have called for me," Jean-Joseph said. "I would have put my foot down."

He sees my inability to end things with Jules as weakness.
He's right.

"I didn't think," she said softly.

"I hate to say it, *chérie*, but that's often your problem, is it not?"

Has he been talking to my mother?

A strange woman wrapped in a ragged cardigan appeared from one of the vineyard rows, her eyes darting maniacally before she disappeared into the vineyard.

Without knowing how she knew, Katrine was sure the

woman was one of the prostitutes who lived in the *Mégisseries*.

What is she doing here?

Just as she was trying to decide whether she should tell Jean-Joseph about the woman Katrine stopped walking, her heart in her throat. Theo stood directly in her path. He looked unsteady on his feet, and he was staring directly at her.

"Not this way," Katrine whispered to Jean-Joseph.

"Why ever not? I thought we were going to get pizza at—"

"Not this way!" Katrine said sharply as Theo began to stumble toward them.

"Katrine!" Theo called to her. "Katrine!"

Jean-Joseph snapped his head around to look at Theo who was lumbering toward them.

"Who the hell is that?" Jean-Joseph said in astonishment.

"I can't...I...I can't!" Katrine said, whirling around, her throat thickening with terror.

She ran, knocking into a young man and spilling the two cups of wine in his hands.

She heard Jean-Joseph and Theo both calling for her as she ran.

As I made my way back into the center of activity of the festival, I saw that the wind had picked up and was blowing in sharp angry gusts that flapped the little flags and paper table coverings of the food tables.

I felt better after solving at least one person's problems by the quick recovery of a small and very naughty collie puppy. Once we'd found her dog, little Amelie scampered off to join her family—her furry bundle of determined escape-artist clutched to her chest—and I retraced my steps to where the noise and music still throbbed in the late afternoon light.

I spotted Marco first. He was standing at one of the wine dispensing tables, his head hanging as if to scrutinize his shoes. Eloise stood opposite him. She was doing all the talking.

I felt sorry for Marco but this wasn't my problem to fix. I could have told him that Eloise was a handful—and possibly on a few nights after too much rosé I did tell him—but he'd enjoyed the relationship for five good months so this was on him to sort out.

Didn't mean I wanted to witness it though.

I moved into the thick of the crowd, louder and more exuberant than when I'd broken free moments when I did my good Samaritan bit. I could see that quite a few of the villagers were feeling no pain.

Alcohol wasn't hard to get during the worst of times around the village but during a harvest festival? There were wine kegs everywhere. I'd been warned by the sisters that much of the wine at the festival might taste more like grape juice if grape juice tasted like lighter fluid. Obviously a lot of the villagers weren't that picky. Singing had already broken out and I saw two men laying out rough wooden planks so that people could dance.

What I *didn't* see was any sign of Katrine which was just as well since I'm not sure our last conversation could be improved upon. Or I don't know what I could have done differently. I still wasn't willing to give up on our friendship but I was starting to believe it would take a lot more time than I'd originally thought.

I saw frenetic movement out of the corner of my eye and when I turned I saw Léa waving to me, a frown on her face.

I went over to where she and Justine were sitting in lawn chairs beside their table of blackberry wine bottles. Several of the bottles I'd carefully packed in boxes this morning were missing. I didn't know whether the twins had sold them or shared them. Five other old ladies were seated next to them. All were sipping wine from ceramic cups. One was smoking.

"Where have you been?" Léa asked and then, without waiting for my answer, "Did you ask Detective Matteo about the permit for next week's market in Aix?"

Okay, so this was the first I'd heard of any permit—or at least about my role in acquiring one via Adrien Matteo, Luc's second-in-command.

The fact that Léa was springing this on me here and not asking Luc for the permit—which would have been a lot easier to do—alerted me to the likelihood that whatever she was up to was probably not legal.

How sweet that she doesn't want to implicate Luc in her scheme, I thought. *Only me.*

There was also the possibility that she didn't think Luc would give the permit to her. All of these thoughts ran in my head but none of them mattered because if I knew one thing about Léa I knew she wanted what she wanted and details be damned.

"Is he expecting my request?" I asked, fully expecting and receiving a look of disdain.

"We need it before the morning, *chérie*," Justine said sweetly. "Thibault is taking five cases of our blackberry wine with him."

Thibault Theroux is a good friend of mine who even

when he is asleep in his bed is not even remotely innocent and certainly not law-abiding.

I turned to scan the crowd but didn't see Detective Matteo the twins' intended pigeon anywhere. With Luc out of town, I figured the Lieutenant was probably dividing his time between patrolling the festival with Eloise and keeping an eye on the village.

Great, I thought with annoyance. *Which means I have to go into Chabanel to find him.*

I looked at the twins to argue but they'd already turned back to their friends, clearly assuming their demands, er, wishes would be followed.

"Fine," I said, feeling my stomach growl and realizing I'd been at the festival three full hours and had eaten very little, let alone enjoyed a glass of lighter fluid wine. I scooped up a cold wedge of *pissaladier* from our table and wolfed it down —*not a pretty look for me but Luc wasn't here so what did I care?*—and headed for the nearest path in the direction of town.

I checked on Roulette first since he was grazing nearby and found him happy enough and his hobbles secure and I was about to take the nearest major walkway—the one that dissected the vineyard and had obviously been used in the old days by tractors to get the bushels of grapes out at harvest time—when I saw Katrine and Jean-Joseph directly in my path.

I didn't think either of us was ready for Round Two so I course-corrected to make my way to the village the long way around the party.

I turned down the first row that had no kiddies playing in it or some old fellow relieving his bladder. As I was gauging the time it was going to take me to get to the village, find Matteo and get back, I quickened my step—as if that would get me back to the party *and food* that much quicker.

I was busy looking over the tops of the grape vines for the quickest way out of the maze when I fell over something underfoot and came crashing down onto the soft ground. I caught my fall with my hands and groaned as the impact reverberated up my arms.

A curse formed on my lips at whatever no-count, selfish fool had left their stupid garbage bag or whatever it was in the middle of a vineyard.

Pushing myself to my knees, I noticed that my favorite boot cut jeans now had two matching mud stains on both knees.

Have I mentioned how difficult it is to launder clothes in post-apocalyptic France?

I turned to give the offending garbage bag a good kick or a piece of my mind when I noticed it wasn't a garbage bag at all.

But a man's body.

12

MURPHY'S LAW

My mouth fell open as I stared at the body and a trembling fear began to course through my arms and legs.

He lay on his back. I could tell by looking at his open but vacant eyes—and the gaping and bloody slash across his throat—that he was not alive.

Even so, I crept to him on my knees and my hand touched his chest.

And then I recoiled in horror.

It was René Deroy.

Confusion flooded my senses for a moment. I stood up on shaky legs and turned in the direction of the festival not far away, twenty yards at most.

Someone had killed him here at the festival.

I glanced nervously about me. Was the murderer still here?

For a moment I was swamped with indecision. Should I go for help? Should I leave him? Should I go on to the village in search of Matteo?

But then I got an image of little Amelie and her naughty

puppy and the very thought that she might come upon Deroy with that horrendous wound in his neck was unthinkable.

I wiped my damp palms against my jeans and took a few steps away from the body, scanning the perimeter of the festival for anyone whose attention I might snag.

And then the luck of the angels fell into my lap! I saw Marco talking to his boss Theo behind the *charcuterie* kiosk, not fifty yards away.

"Marco!" I screamed. I saw him look up and frown as if he'd heard something but couldn't tell from where.

"Marco!" I screamed again and this time he snapped his head in my direction. I waved desperately and saw him pat Theo on the shoulder and make his excuses before turning to walk toward me.

There's something immediate and exquisite about the process of transferring the responsibility of an untenable situation. As soon as Marco joined me in the clearing and his look of puzzlement changed to shock when he saw Deroy's body, I felt like this crisis was no longer mine alone to handle.

"Is Matteo here?" I asked.

Marco stared at the body, an incredulous gaze on his face.

"Marco!" I said. "Snap out of it! We need to get Matteo or Eloise!"

"Is he…is he…?"

"Yes, he is. Do *you* want to go for the police or do you want me to?" I said.

Please say I should go.

"I'll go," he said. "Detective Matteo is by the bakery table." He turned without another word and dashed back to the festival.

Fifteen minutes later, the shaking had nearly stopped in my hands and arms and both Matteo and Eloise were leaning over the body. Marco had come to stand next to me and I felt his strong warm hands rubbing my back.

Detective Matteo knelt by the body and I did my best not to look at it. I'm not quite sure why I was so squeamish because I've seen dead bodies before.

But this guy had been alive—and in my house—not twelve hours earlier.

"Do you know him?" Eloise asked me, her notepad out.

"He spent the night at *La Fleurette* last night," I said.

"Jules!" Marco said, agony in his voice.

I gave him a sharp look. "I'm not going to lie. He was at my house but I caught him stealing and so I threw him out."

"Wait a minute," Eloise said, turning to Matteo. "Is this the guy who was fighting with Deschamps earlier?"

Matteo didn't answer.

"He and Monsieur Deschamps traded punches," Marco said, chewing his lip as he looked at the body on the ground.

That must have been the noise I'd heard before I ran off to solve Amelie's lost puppy problem.

A few people wandered over from the food and music tents to where we were standing.

"What's happened?" one of the villagers asked.

"Keep them back!" Matteo snapped at Eloise.

"Hey, that's the man who was assaulted by the American!" said one villager, a ruddy-faced pensioner.

"What are you talking about?" Eloise asked, brandishing her stupid notebook and pen once more.

"I met him as I was setting up my stand," the old man said. "He told me the American attacked him with a claw hammer this morning when he was sleeping in a ditch outside Chabanel."

"Well, that's not true," I said, stung. I looked into the old man's face and saw no obvious malice. He probably just bumped into Deroy who was trying to get his version out of what happened last night before I got mine out.

"Yes, I talked to him too," a stout woman said, her beady eyes on me. "I gave him a bun with some coffee and he said *les soeurs* gave him a bed for the night and then the American showed up and told him to get out of the village or she'd kill him."

Four other people who'd gathered at the murder scene gasped on cue at this damning pronouncement.

"How dare she threaten to throw him out of Chabanel!" another woman said. "He has more right to be here since he is French and she is not!"

I'm not saying there's a whole lot of anti-American sentiment in the village but there is some. Most people assume that the dirty bomb that went off over the Mediterranean was triggered by something the Americans must have done. And since the US wasn't seriously affected by the fall-out of the bomb everyone just viewed it as another example of the US doing what it wants while everyone else pays the price.

"Jules Hooker Alaoui," Eloise said, her voice breathy with excitement and determination. "You are under arrest for the murder of…"

"Oh, come on now!" I said. "That's ridiculous! I didn't kill him. Detective Matteo?"

Matteo stood up, his hands on his hips, and continued to study the body before turning to us.

"I will protect the crime scene," he said. "Sergeant Basile, you may take the prisoner in for questioning."

"I will not let you do it!" Marco said hotly to Eloise.

But really? You don't have to be the brightest bulb in the pack to know that this was *not* the thing to say right then. Eloise probably already believed *I* was the reason her relationship with Marco had fallen apart.

She turned on him, spittle flying from her lips that were pulled back from bared teeth.

Yep. I'm going to go out on a limb here and say Marco must have finally got the words out to break up with her.

Great timing. Lucky me.

"Stand back," Eloise snarled at him. "Or I'll bring you in too."

Before Eloise could get her handcuffs out of her jacket pocket, one of the people in the crowd yelled out, "Look there! Is that the murder weapon?"

All of us turned to see where he was pointing and there in the bushes not three feet from Deroy's body was the gleam of what looked like a green-handled utility knife.

Matteo went to it, took out his handkerchief and gingerly picked it up.

"Hey, that's my knife!" I said before I realized what I was saying.

As Eloise turned me around and snapped the cuffs on my wrists I heard Marco groan in defeat.

13

CLOSING RANKS

So, are we all on the same page now?
It didn't take a mental giant to figure that Eloise had less to nothing to warrant locking me up but of course holding me for murder wasn't her main purpose.

Her main purpose was to get back at Marco and secondarily at me for the terrible crime I'd committed against her.

So fine. She was in a position of power and she used it. Nothing new here, folks. When Luc got back, I'd be released straight away. I was mildly surprised that Matteo let her take me to jail in the first place.

Matteo isn't my most favorite person in the world but he's logical and sometimes humane. My guess is he needed Eloise to move the growing circus of onlookers *away* from the crime scene and saw my arrest as a good way to do that.

I don't appreciate being used but since it's the sort of thing *I'd* have done, I have to sort of respect it.

After the ruckus of being led through the vineyard to the police station in the village with the accompaniment of what felt like half the village, Eloise slammed the door to the hallway, cutting off the noise of the rabble. Silence enveloped me.

I sat on the single cot in the cell, glad for the small window that let in enough light for me not to be in total darkness. The light faded pretty quickly in Provence in October so I wasn't hopeful of having much of it as the rest of the day dwindled away. But I did have hope that Luc would be back before nightfall.

Unless he decided to spend the night in Nice.

I wrapped up in the thin wool blanket from the bed and listened to the hum of voices coming from the other room. I hoped the twins would go home and that Marco would go with them. First, they'd need him to load and unload the cart and secondly, Marco's presence here at the police station was a red flag to a bull as far as Eloise was concerned.

Although at present I couldn't think of what more she could do to me.

I must have dozed off because when I came to, it was totally dark in the cell and there were no more voices in the other room. I was hoping to talk to Matteo about what he'd found at the crime scene but then reasoned that since I was being held under suspicion of murder he probably wouldn't tell me anyway.

I glanced at my watch. It was after two in the morning.

Luc wasn't coming back tonight. Disappointed and feeling more than a little abandoned, I lay down on the mattress and eventually drifted off to sleep.

The next morning I was awakened by the scent of brewing coffee and screaming.

Not unlike my mornings at *La Fleurette* now that I think about it.

"Matteo said I could because he saw what I saw!" Eloise shouted. "She killed a man under our very noses!"

I swung my legs off the cot and stared at the hall until Luc appeared.

Dear God, he's handsome. His hair was a thick dark brown, and his eyes—grey and concerned—seemed to bore right through me. In one hand he held a mug of steaming coffee and in the other, the keys to my cell. He must have left Nice before dawn to get here this early.

"Good morning, *chérie*," he said, as he opened the cell door. "Will you have your Americano in your cell or my office?"

"Office," I said, getting to my feet and taking the coffee mug. I wondered about the protocol of kissing him but decided against it.

I dropped the blanket on the cot and followed him down the hall and past a seething Eloise.

Her animosity toward me was nearly palpable.

I glanced past her at Madame Gabin who was once more at her receptionist's desk.

"Do you know if *les soeurs* got the horse harnessed last night?" I asked her.

"I believe they and the horse are home safe and sound," she said, arching an eyebrow at me.

I followed Luc into his office. He shut the door behind me, took my coffee from me and set it on his desk, then took me into his arms.

You know how it is when you're being brave but as soon as someone says something kind to you, you break down? Yeah, like that.

The feeling of Luc's arms around me, so strong and comforting, told me in no uncertain terms that the bad times were over and all would be well.

Maybe he'd even fire Eloise?

I must say I'd fantasized about that a good bit the night before when I wasn't imagining her being run out of town covered with tar but of course if he sacked her then I'd have to worry about the crazy hag firebombing my house.

"I didn't kill him," I murmured into his jacket. It smelled of tweed and lemons and cigarette smoke.

"Of course you didn't," he said gruffly, settling me down on a chair across from his desk. I picked up the coffee mug and drank deeply. It was delicious with just a hint of cinnamon and cardamom.

"Deroy spent the night with us at *La Fleurette* and must have stolen my knife."

Luc sat down at his desk and picked up his own coffee.

"I heard he was going around bad-mouthing me after that," I said.

Luc's eyes watched me over the rim of his coffee mug. "So what's going on between you and Eloise?"

"Well, Marco broke up with her yesterday. And she thinks I'm the reason or something."

"Ah."

"I can't believe I had to spend the night in a cell!"

"I'm pretty annoyed about it myself."

He didn't *look* annoyed but still waters were practically stagnant with Luc and trust me they ran way deep. I wouldn't want to be Eloise this morning.

"Why did Deroy spend the night at *La Fleurette*?" Luc asked.

"I found him limping along the side of the road. He said

he was hurt and starving so I offered him a place to sleep for the night."

"Of course you did."

"Luc, you would have done the same. In fact I've *seen* you do the same!"

"Yes, but I am not ninety-five years old or a woman. Plus I'm usually armed."

"Well, the twins are too, as you know. In fact, when we caught him prowling around our living room in the middle of the night with a bag of our stuff, Léa ushered him out the door at the tip of her MAS-36."

Luc bit back a grin. "I keep meaning to take that away from her." Then he reached across the desk and took my hand.

"You are all right? No worse for wear?"

"Good American idiom," I said. "You've been studying."

"I missed you."

"And me, you. Are you going to fire Eloise?"

His face tightened and he released my hand. I cursed myself for bringing her up. It had been so nice up to then.

"Do you need a ride home?" he asked. He was already looking around his desk and I knew how busy he must be, especially since he'd been out of town the day before and now he had a murder on his plate. I don't know what else happened in Chabanel besides the murder but with the festival there were probably a few other things that would need to be sorted out.

"No worries," I said, although the prospect of the two-mile walk home was not a happy one.

"Thibault is outside. I'm sure he can give you a ride."

The mention of Thibault reminded me of the permit the twins wanted and while a normal person might not be expected to still need to perform certain chores if they've been arrested and spent the night in jail I knew *les soeurs'* expectations extended to the assumption that their original request would be fulfilled.

"Is Matteo anywhere in the office today?" I asked wearily.

14

HOLDING ALL THE CARDS

Luc watched Jules climb into Thibault Theroux's car and felt his stomach muscles tighten involuntarily. He hoped he'd made it clear to her that she was not a suspect. But it was still a mess, he thought—mostly stemming from Eloise's determination to make someone pay for her heartache.

Luc's second-in-command Adrien Matteo stuck his head in the doorway.

"Are you free, Chief?"

Luc waved him in but first he stepped into the hallway and addressed Madame Gabin at the front desk.

"Madame Gabin, please have Sergeant Basile see me when she returns from her rounds."

"Of course, Chief."

Luc walked back to his office and closed the door.

Matteo was waiting for him to take a seat before sitting himself. Adrien Matteo was a strange man, Luc thought, and not for the first time.

Very formal with a marked inability to see the gray areas in most situations. If it weren't for the manpower shortage in the police service, Luc would have cut him loose months ago. But finding any able man these days to serve was nearly impossible. The pay had been eliminated within weeks of the EMP—substituted by housing and food chits—and the work was long and arduous, made worse by the lack of electricity, functioning weapons and reliable communications.

"All right," Luc said, sitting down. "What do we have?"

Matteo flipped open his notebook. "White male, late thirties, identified as one René Deroy. Died of massive blood loss due to a severe laceration to the throat. The ME has taken the body to Aix and will get back to us with a better approximation of time of death."

"I understand you broke up a fight with the victim and a Monsieur Deschamps? A garlic farmer out by the eastern highway?"

"Correct. No real damage sustained by either party. Witnesses say Deschamps attacked Deroy."

"Does Deschamps say why?"

"He is unforthcoming at this time."

"We'll need to make him more forthcoming," Luc said ominously.

Matteo's eyes glittered at the inflection from his boss but it was hard for Luc to determine whether the man would like to *force* Deschamps to talk or whether he was merely thinking of compiling more evidence against Luc.

Luc knew very well that Matteo would be happy to see the back of him. The man had been caught several times revealing information that was just shy of classified to people he shouldn't be telling. Like Chabanel's last mayor, for one.

It was that *just shy of* category that had saved him, Luc thought. *So far.*

"And the murder weapon?" Luc asked.

Matteo held up a plastic bag with the utility knife inside. The blade was stained red.

"Found in the bushes three feet from the body," Matteo said. "Jules Hooker has identified it as hers."

"Well, she said she has one like it," Luc said, feeling a throb of annoyance in his temple.

"We'll check the prints to see if hers match and otherwise if she recants her confession—"

"I think you mean her assertion."

"Yes, her assertion that the weapon is hers. Otherwise she'll need to bring her own knife in to prove this isn't it."

"And the reason you felt comfortable allowing Eloise to take Jules into custody?" Now Luc felt anger pinching into his veins and he worked hard not to let it show.

"Why, to defuse the situation, of course," Matteo said blandly, watching Luc's face for his reaction. "And because there were two witnesses at the scene maintaining they overheard her threaten the victim with bodily harm."

"Are you sure? Wasn't it really the case that they overheard *Deroy* claiming that Jules threatened him?"

Matteo flipped through his notebook and then looked back up, his expression impassive.

"I don't have that information. I didn't have time to write down their statements at the time," he said, a tic twitching in his left eyebrow. "But I have their names."

"Fine. Anything else?"

Matteo glanced at his notes. "There appeared to be lipstick on the victim's mouth. The ME will confirm tomorrow."

"The victim was wearing lipstick?"

"No. It was smudged as if he'd...been kissed."

A flash of discomfort invaded Luc's gut.

Jules always wore lipstick and very few women in the village still did these days.

A tapping at his door prompted Matteo to get up and open it.

"You wanted to see me, Chief?" Eloise said, stepping into the room. Because lipstick was on his mind, Luc noticed that Eloise herself had a light blush of color on her mouth.

So at least Jules won't be hung on her lipstick alone.

"Come in," he said tersely but he did not offer her a seat. "That's all, Detective," he said to Matteo who quickly exited the room.

Eloise crossed her arms and stood in front of Luc's desk.

"You were out of line putting Jules Hooker in a cell for the night," Luc said.

"I can see why you might think that."

"I understand you're upset but I won't have your personal problems spilling over into your work. You would have done better taking statements of the people at the festival than what you did. The real killer caught a lucky break because *you* allowed your personal feelings to interfere."

"So you've already decided that Jules isn't the real killer?" Eloise asked.

"She isn't the real killer and you know it."

"Oh? And do you know that because you're allowing *your* personal feelings to interfere?"

Luc stood up. "You're off this case, Eloise. This is clearly personal for you and is affecting your professional objectivity. Take some time off to sort yourself out."

"And you feel comfortable letting me off in the middle of a murder investigation? I thought all hands were needed."

"All *able* hands."

"I see. Well, I'm afraid you won't be allowed to do that, Chief."

He looked at her with incredulity.

"You're lucky I don't fire you on the spot! Gross misconduct! Using your office to promote a personal vendetta—"

"You mean like *she* did to *me* last summer when she tricked me into bringing her to Grighot?" Eloise said, her face flushing. "When she *promised* she'd set Marco free and all along she had no intention of doing it? And now he's *dumped* me?"

Luc's shoulders sagged. "Eloise, look. I know this is hard and I'm sorry about you and Marco—"

"Save it, sir. I don't need your pity and I'm *not* sitting this one out. Not when it's *you* who's biased."

"Sergeant, you need to stand down right now before you say something you'll regret," Luc said, his hands on his hips.

"I'm not taking orders from you about this case," Eloise said hotly. "Not as soon as the impartial investigator I asked headquarters to send arrives to take it over from you."

"What are you talking about?"

"You know what *impartial* means, don't you, Chief?" Eloise turned on her heel and walked to the door before giving a parting shot over her shoulder.

"It means someone who's not sleeping with our lead suspect!"

15

STAYING ALIVE

There's something about an evening meal in France that puts any other time or place to shame. Maybe I think that because I'm usually sharing my evening meal with people I consider family and if you came from a family like mine back in the States, you'd see what a miracle that is.

At *La Fleurette* we always eat in the kitchen unless it's warm enough to eat outdoors. These days, meals enjoyed in the garden are just a pleasant memory.

I took my seat at the kitchen table and pulled my sweater tighter around me. Even in a room anchored by a big iron stove that was almost always blazing, it was chilly in the room.

I was weary this evening. While I'd only recently been released from the Big House my celebratory homecoming involved still needing to feed the livestock and collect the potatoes from the garden for dinner. Fortunately Marco was on hand to chop the kindling and drag firewood to the kitchen.

The four of us briefly held hands at the kitchen table

while Léa and Justine murmured grace. Twig—who had run away from Eloise and found his way back to *La Fleurette*—was under the table with Cocoa. One of the cats—Neige—sat on the wide stone kitchen windowsill glaring at us. It wasn't clear what his problem was. I could see he had a full bowl of chicken gizzards on the floor.

I'm not sure who the unfortunate chicken was who joined us for tonight's meal—Justine is always scolding me for making pets out of them—but I've never been more grateful than when Léa spooned out the redolent chicken pieces into my bowl and poured that amazing sauce of garlicky wine and onions over the top. You may call it *coq au vin*. I call it heaven in a bowl.

"It is unbelievable that Sergeant Basile would act as she did," Justine said, shaking her head as she passed me the bread.

"Do you think so?" Léa said, and then gave a deliberate side glance at Marco.

She had a point. It was pretty obvious that Marco's timing in breaking up with Eloise was the reason she went after me.

"So I take it you did finally break up with her?" I asked as I slipped pieces of bread under the table to each of the waiting dogs.

He nodded morosely. "I am sorry, Jules."

"No, it had to be done," I said reaching for my glass of wine. After the first sip I looked at the twins in surprise. "This is real wine!"

"Our blackberry wine is not fake wine," Léa said.

"Monsieur Theroux brought two bottles when he dropped you off," Justine said. "He is so *gentil*, always thinking of others."

Yeah, especially his partners in crime, I thought.

"So is this the beginning of there being more wine available, do you think?" I asked.

Léa shook her head. "Most of the wine from vineyards around here will go to the black market. Unless you know someone to hold back bottles for you…" She shrugged as if to indicate the French version of *you're outta luck*.

"And I guess Thibault is our *someone*?" I said, taking another sip. "Mm-mm. Lucky us."

"Madame Tulle said she saw Marie Dionne at the *fête*," Justine said.

I don't know half the people the twins talk about so I was pretty sure she wasn't addressing me.

"I saw her there," Léa said. "She skulked around the kiosks like the wanton slut that she is."

Whoa! That got my attention.

"Who is Marie Dionne?" I asked.

"She lives in the *Mégisseries*," Justine said, referring to the outskirts of the village where most of the poor live along with petty criminals and sex workers.

"And she doesn't normally come to the village festivals?" I asked.

"You are very amusing, Jules," Léa said in a voice that meant the exact opposite.

Neige chose that moment to jump on the table and was quickly batted down by Léa as if she'd been waiting for the cat to make its move.

"What do you think she was doing there?" Marco asked.

The twins didn't bother answering him. If she really was a prostitute, she was probably there to drum up business.

"Did you see Madame Pelletier?" Léa asked me, changing the subject.

"Yes but we had words," I said. "And not good words."

"Why does she not forgive you?" Marco said spearing a piece of potato in his broth. "Is that not what friends do?"

"I'm pretty sure she will in time. Which reminds me, what's going on with Theo?"

Marco frowned. "What do you mean?"

"He was drunk as a skunk today," I glanced at the twins to see if they'd noticed too. They were both nodding.

"He was?" Marco put another serving of the aromatic stewed chicken on his plate. Neige went back to his place on the windowsill and began cleaning a paw as if his altercation with Léa had never happened.

"Men!" I said with a laugh. "You seriously haven't noticed that Theo is wasted almost all the time these days?"

He shrugged, his mouth full.

"I do not think Madame Pelletier will forgive you," Léa said.

I looked at her and reminded myself that Léa Cazaly was a *glass-is-mostly-empty-and-probably-broken* kind of girl.

"I'm afraid I don't think so either, *chérie*," Justine said, ending whatever solace I was taking from considering Léa-as-source. "She stood right there when you were being arrested and didn't look at all concerned."

"She should be honored to be your friend," Marco said.

"At least she doesn't hate you as Sergeant Basile does," Léa said.

"You must be careful, *chérie*," Justine said earnestly. "Eloise is in a position to make your life very hard."

Tell me about it. I still had a bruise on my hip from that rock hard jail-cell mattress.

"Luc will keep her in line," I said. "And he'll make sure Deroy's murder isn't laid at my feet."

"I do not know about that," Léa said, standing up and starting to clear the table. "Thibault said he overheard

Sergeant Basile make a formal request to have an impartial investigator come to Chabanel to review the case."

My mouth suddenly felt dry.

"Well, see?" I said, gulping more wine. "That's exactly what we need. Someone impartial, without an axe to grind."

The three of them looked at me and frowned.

"Monsieur Deroy was not killed with an axe," Léa said.

"No, it's an American idiom," I said. "It means—"

"He was killed with *your* knife, *chérie*," Justine said with a disapproving look as if I'd deliberately left my tool around to be picked up my criminals who would later be careless enough to be killed by them.

"Yeah," I said with a heavy sigh. "That's not good."

After dinner Marco and I washed and dried the dishes while *les soeurs* retired to the front salon with their sewing and knitting. For someone who'd just broken up with his girlfriend of five months, he seemed pretty jolly to me, but that's Marco. He was always seeing the bright side of things and I couldn't help but think that was a pretty healthy way to go through life.

"So tell me about this fight Deroy had at the festival with one of the farmers," I said. "Did you see it?"

Marco squinted at a wine glass as though he could still detect soap bubbles on it but eventually just dried it.

"*Oui*," he said. "Detective Matteo broke it up before anyone got hurt."

"I wonder why they were fighting. I wonder if Deroy knew the farmer beforehand?"

"I do not know."

"Well, obviously, the police will talk to him. What's his name?"

"I do not know this either. You think the *farmer* killed Monsieur Deroy?"

"Makes more sense than *me* killing him."

Marco handed me the perfectly dried wine glass and I put it away in the open shelf over the sink.

"Are you sure Chief DeBray will not listen to Eloise about the evidence against you?" Marco asked. "She is very angry with me. Perhaps I should go back with her? Just until the case is solved?"

I put a hand on his shoulder and he turned to look at me.

"I get that Luc has to play by the rules and not give me special treatment but he's not going to let Eloise indulge some personal vendetta. It took you too long to finally break up with her. You're not going back with her. Period."

"But what about the investigator that is coming?"

For the first time I saw strain in his face. It had been a rough couple of weeks for him. Eloise had not made the break-up easy and he was a sweet man who cared deeply about his friends. Heck, when I'd needed a favor he *married* me.

"I'm not worried about it, Marco. So don't *you* be. Okay? It's all going to be fine. I promise."

He nodded. But I could see he was still worried.

16

RHAPSODY IN BLOOD

Marie wasn't sure she could get out of bed.

She lay there trembling and listened to the voices outside the small shed where she lived. Always before she considered herself lucky to have her own space. Most of the other women were happy enough to share a house. They welcomed the camaraderie.

Like one big dormitory, she thought bitterly. *And we're all just girls waiting for our big break. As if this life isn't the only one there ever was going to be for any of us.*

The rough laughter outside seemed to shimmy against the walls of the shed. Two men, maybe more stood there, if not on her doorstep, then near it. Waiting. Wanting.

She didn't have to answer the door. There were plenty who'd take them if she wouldn't.

She just couldn't. Not today. Not yet.

Her stomach lurched as the image of René crept unbidden into her head. He was sprawled on his back, his face staring up into the sky.

He had looked so surprised. As if he was shocked that anyone would want to kill him.

Marie's stomach wouldn't settle and she forced herself into a sitting position hoping that might help. The thin wool blanket across her legs fell to the floor when she moved.

She reached for it and saw her hand, withered and deformed. It looked worse now than when it had happened. She pulled the blanket back onto her lap.

How could he be so surprised?

He should only have been surprised that it had taken so long.

The words seemed to calm her stomach and she leaned back in bed. She called to mind René's dead face again. And felt a slight shiver of satisfaction.

17

HALF BAKED

The next morning Luc was at the station before anyone else except Madame Gabin. He wasn't exactly sure how things had been left when he and Eloise parted last night but he wouldn't be surprised to see her today. If she forced his hand, he'd have to strip her of her badge and send her home.

He didn't want to do that for many reasons, not the least of which was that Eloise had always been a friend and that would end the friendship for good. But also he didn't want to push this situation too far because an investigation into his relationship with Jules might not result in anyone's favor either.

The fact was Jules *had* found the body. She'd even admitted to threatening the victim with bodily harm—at gun point—although granted Léa Cazaly was the one holding the gun—and in all likelihood it would be shown that the victim was killed with *Jules'* knife.

On the face of it she appeared to have motive, opportunity and method all neatly nailed.

Luc had no doubt that Jules had nothing to do with

Deroy's death but if he didn't go through the official steps, careful not to miss a single one, they would all suffer down the line.

As for this "independent investigator" that Eloise swore was coming to take over the case, Luc had thus far received no communications that that was happening.

He drank the coffee Madame Gabin had made and looked through the window at the front of the station. The sun would warm the day but right now the square that the station faced appeared a cheerless, windswept place of cracked pavers and scrubby grass.

It had taken all his strength not to go to Jules last night but even he knew that would be asking for trouble. People were watching. This was a small village. People were always watching. The more he ran this case by the rules—strictly by the rules—the better for everyone, and the faster he'd find the real killer.

Outside he saw a figure appear from across the square. Matteo walked stiffly as though he was in some kind of pain. Luc didn't normally work closely with Matteo but today he'd have to. He steeled himself to ignore the man's peccadilloes in order to stay focused on finding the clues that would lead them to absolving Jules and finding René Deroy's murderer as quickly as possible.

"We have time for coffee," Luc said as Matteo stepped up the slick, broad stone steps of the police station.

"Not necessary," Matteo said. "I'm ready."

Did the man not even drink coffee?

With Eloise out on administrative leave and by partnering with Matteo today they would be shorthanded.

"Were you able to get in touch with Romeo?" Lux asked Madame Gabin.

"Yes, Chief. He's coming in mid-morning."

Romeo Remey had worked part-time in the office until last spring when he finally decided to retire but he was generally available if needed.

"Very good. Detective?" He turned to Matteo and the two of them descended the steps to Luc's car, a vintage CV2.

He had no doubt it was going to be a long day.

Their first visit was to the farm of Michel Deschamps. Luc knew the farmer only slightly since the man rarely came to the village. Deschamps had a young second wife and a teenage daughter.

"Wife, Belle," Matteo read off his notepad. "Daughter, thirteen. Angelique."

"Remind me what happened to his first wife," Luc said as he drove down the long pot-hole pocked road that turned into a dirt road before winding through several unkempt hectares of vineyards.

"Cancer," Matteo said. "No children."

Luc parked in the wide gravel driveway. The house wasn't big enough to be considered a *mas* like *La Fleurette* but it was a large country house nonetheless.

"No money problems?" Luc asked as he climbed out of the car.

"Not that I know of. He grows garlic. And keeps to himself."

They stepped onto the stone terrace in front of the farmhouse. Luc noticed that the terrace had been recently swept. He knocked on the door and heard dogs barking inside.

A calico curtain hung from a small window in the door and Luc watched a corner of it twitch back to reveal two eyes.

"Luc DeBray, Chief of Chabanel police," he said. "And

Detective Adrien Matteo. We're here to see Monsieur Deschamps."

The door swung open suddenly and Michel Deschamps stood in the doorway, his brow knitted together in irritation.

"I didn't kill him," Deschamps said. "You have no proof that I did."

"We just want to ask you a few questions, Monsieur Deschamps," Luc said. "May we come in?"

Deschamps stepped out onto the terrace and shut the door firmly behind him.

I guess that answers that question.

"I understand you and René Deroy had a disagreement yesterday at the festival," Luc said.

Deschamps' eyes flicked to Matteo because Matteo was the one who'd broken up the fight.

"I punched him. Doesn't mean I killed him."

"What was the fight over?"

"None of your business."

"I have a dead body in my village," Luc said between gritted teeth. "So it is very much my business. I'll ask you again."

"He made a pass at my wife."

That was a surprise and by the way Matteo cleared his throat, obviously he thought so too.

"Is Madame Deschamps at home?" Luc asked.

"She's busy."

"Fine. You can bring her down to the station then."

Deschamps snorted and opened the door behind him. He turned toward the interior of the house and shouted "Belle!"

A plain woman in her mid-thirties appeared. She looked terrified.

"Tell them why I punched that bastard at the festival," Deschamps said to her.

She looked at him, her eyes wide and blinking.

"Go on! Tell them why I hit him!"

The woman gripped the apron around her waist, her eyes darting everywhere in obvious fear.

"*Belle!*" Deschamps barked.

"Quit shouting at her," Matteo said. There was a tone of calm menace in Matteo's voice that surprised Luc.

"I...I...the man tried to steal a kiss," Belle said, her eyes dropping to the ground.

"I see," Luc said, frowning. "Madame Deschamps, do you wear lipstick?"

"She wasn't asking for it if that's what you're implying," Deschamps sneered.

"Do you or do you not wear lipstick?" Luc asked again, trying to ignore the hulking farmer in front of him.

"I don't," she said in a small voice. "Never."

"I was with my family every moment since the fight," Deschamps said. "Ask her. I was never out of her sight. Isn't that right, Belle? Tell him."

"Yes, that's right. He was with me every minute."

An alibi all primed and ready in his back pocket, Luc thought. *How convenient.*

"Are we done?" Deschamps said.

"For now."

The farmer stepped back into the house and slammed the door. Luc and Matteo hesitated a moment and then turned and walked back to the car.

"Do you believe her?" Matteo asked. "About the lipstick?"

"I believe she would say whatever her husband told her to say."

"Do you think Deroy stole his kiss and that's what was on his face? Her lipstick?"

"Have we heard back from the lab or the ME yet?"

Matteo shook his head. They reached the car and turned to stare back at the house.

"Everything would be so much easier if people would just not lie to us at every opportunity," Matteo said with a sigh.

And that was the third time this morning that Matteo had surprised Luc. Luc had been so used to believing that his detective was a robot that these little glimmers of humanity and personality were down right startling.

"Deschamps had opportunity *and* motive," Luc said.

"To kill over a kiss? Not much in the way of motive. And what about the murder weapon? How did he get that?"

"Jules said Deroy stole the knife from her. He could have pulled it on Deschamps, had it taken away from him and used against him."

"It's possible."

"Does Deschamps strike you as the impulsive type?"

Matteo frowned as both men got in the car. "Quick to anger, surely."

"Whoever killed Deroy did it quickly, quietly and with at least one hundred people not fifty yards away."

"Yes, but most of those people were a little worse for wear."

"Granted."

"But I take your meaning. Stealth doesn't seem to be our farmer's strong suit."

"True," Luc said grimly. "But that doesn't mean he didn't do it."

∽

Angelique Deschamps crouched in the upstairs bedroom window and watched the policemen walk back to their car. She'd known better than to come downstairs when she heard the knock at the door.

She felt a thickness in her throat as she remembered what happened in the pasture but quickly pushed the memory away.

From where she knelt in her bedroom by the heating vent she'd heard the adults' words as clearly as if she'd been in the same room with them.

She'd heard her father's easy lies to the police, her heart jumping with every word he uttered.

The policemen were leaving now, leaving her and *Maman* with her father.

Her father who had killed a man last night.

18

A WING AND A PRAYER

Eloise saw the Chief's car was not in its usual spot but she also knew that that bulldog Madame Gabin would toss her out if Eloise attempted to go into the police station when everyone knew the Chief had told her *not* to come in today.

Madame Gabin was a silly old woman. She didn't know what Eloise knew—that the Chief was too besotted with the American to see clearly.

From where Eloise sat at Café Sucre, she had a perfect view of the village square. The police station was situated directly across from the World War I memorial statue with the names of the village's dozen war dead. Next to the police station was city hall. As far as Eloise knew, only the mayor's secretary Madame LaTour was inside.

The so-called mayor—Theo Bardot—had been missing in action ever since he'd taken over as the new mayor of Chabanel.

Eloise turned to catch a glimpse of Marco as he darted around the café tables filling orders. He'd been careful not to look at her after depositing an espresso in front of her and scurrying away.

Just looking at him made her heart hurt.

The way his hair flopped over one eye and his grin spread over his entire face. She could remember very well the look in his eye as he regarded her during any of a hundred romantic moments between them.

Those happy memories took an instant nose-dive when she caught his eye now and watched him quickly look away.

And then the American came between us.

Eloise had always known that Jules and Marco's marriage was not a sham—no matter how many times Marco tried to tell her otherwise.

How could it be? Look at him! He's more gorgeous than George Clooney in his prime. Everyone wants him. Even the men look at him twice.

And he had been mine.

A nearly overwhelming urge to run away or to hide from the agony of what she felt threatened to overwhelm her when suddenly she heard the sound of a motorbike.

Motorbikes weren't as rare as cars these days but neither were they an everyday occurrence. All the people in the café began to crane their necks to see who was coming.

Eloise was up on her feet and walking to the front of the police station before the biker materialized on the road. Sure enough, when he appeared, he was heading straight for the police *municipale*.

Eloise quickened her pace. It was important to reach the investigator before he went inside and was immediately poisoned against her by anything that embittered old Madame Gabin had to say.

"Excuse me!" Eloise called out, glad that she'd worn her

uniform today in spite of the Chief's edict. "Are you from police headquarters in Nice?"

The man parked his bike in front of the double doors of the police station and turned to look at her. He was slim, of medium height with dark hair and probing nearly pupilless brown eyes.

He wasn't in uniform, of course, because he was a detective. But the steely look he gave her left no ambiguity that he was an officer of the law. In spite of herself Eloise felt a tingle of excitement as she hurried over to him.

"I am Sergeant Eloise Basile," she said, shaking hands with him. "I am the one who requested you."

"Detective Lieutenant Marc Dobry," he said in clipped, Parisian French. "Is Chief DeBray in?"

Eloise fought down her annoyance that Dobry wanted to leap frog over her to deal straight with the Chief.

"No, he is out canvassing the witnesses in the case," she said as she walked with him up the stairs to the double doors of the police station.

He frowned. "You told him I was coming to take over the case?" He patted his jacket pocket as if to reassure himself that his orders were there.

"I did. But Chief DeBray has his own way of thinking and you'll discover it's not always beneficial to the investigation."

Dobry's eyebrows shot up. "You are saying he is an actual impediment to the investigation? Is this a formal charge?"

"No, no," Eloise said hurriedly. "At least not yet. Let me show you to his office where we can talk until he returns." She ran ahead of him and marched in, relieved to see that Madame Gabin was not at her desk. Eloise led Dobry to the Chief's office.

The man went to Luc's desk and sat down, looking around him as he did.

"Fill me in," he said.

Eloise straightened the creases in her jacket and pointed to the file folder on the Chief's desk. She told Dobry succinctly and without emotion how Jules found the body and admitted to quarreling with the victim as well as owning the murder weapon.

She watched Dobry's eyebrows arch and his full lips form into a frown.

"Is the suspect in custody?" he asked.

"I arrested her but she was released when Chief DeBray returned."

"On what grounds?"

"Personal reasons. The *Chief's* personal reasons."

Dobry snorted and took his papers out of his jacket and tossed them on the desk.

"Well, I can certainly see why you contacted HQ," he said. "And you say he is sleeping with the suspect?"

"That is correct. Or at least, if he's not sleeping with her, he is definitely *with* her. I don't know to what degree…er, if they have…" Eloise blushed.

Dobry waved a hand at her embarrassment. "They are together, is that not so?"

"Yes. They are."

He nodded. "Then of course you were right to call for an independent investigator."

Eloise breathed a sigh of relief. "Thank you, sir."

Dobry tapped a forefinger against his lips as if in thought. "I suppose it is possible your chief felt there wasn't enough evidence to hold the suspect."

Eloise let his words slide over her and forced herself to swallow her feelings of disappointment.

"I suppose so, sir."

"But we will find out the truth."

Dobry flipped opened the file folder and scanned the contents before standing up and walking to the window.

"In the meantime," Eloise said, surreptitiously wiping her damp hands against her uniform trousers, "even if there's not enough evidence to legally hold her right now, I was thinking we could detain her offsite until all the evidence was revealed."

A moment of silence passed between them before Dobry turned and for a moment looked as if he was surprised to still find her there.

"I assume you have some place in mind?"

Eloise felt a feeling of expansion fill her chest. "I do. Yes, sir," she said, barely able to breathe.

"How far is it from here?"

"About seven miles."

"Very good. Very good. *Geisha*, is it?"

It was a moment before the clouds of confusion cleared and Eloise realized what he was asking.

"No, sir," she said. "It's called *Grighot*."

19

HOPE AGAINST HOPE

Matteo hated the *Mégisseries*.

Just because someone had seen a prostitute at the festival was no reason to believe the woman was in any way a suspect.

But he still needed to talk to her.

Had she been looking for business?

The *Mégisseries* was perched at the edge of Chabanel. Its streets consisted of a main drag lined with wooden shacks and stone rubble shelters that had at one time been proper domiciles. Now graffiti and curse words were scrawled across them and trash blew in the streets.

Matteo grimaced at the pervasive smell of mildew, marijuana and wet dog fur.

How do people live like this?

A stooped old man glanced at Matteo from the corner of the street.

"You there!" Matteo called out, pleased to see the old fellow flinch in fear.

Only an idiot believed you actually had to be doing something wrong to end up in jail.

Matteo went to him, his face set in his best policeman's mien.

"I am looking for Marie Dionne," Matteo said. "Where does she live?"

The old man's eyes darted across the street before quickly looking at the ground where he kept his gaze.

"I…I am not sure," he said.

But his reaction had told Matteo enough. Matteo turned from the man and strode to the bank of apartments on the facing street. He was sure that moments ago there had been at least half a dozen people on this street.

Now there were only two elderly women, smoking and watching him.

"Marie Dionne," Matteo said without introduction. "Where does she live?"

The taller woman sucked on her cigarette and looked Matteo up and down as if she had no intention of speaking.

"I have plenty of time," Matteo said. "More than enough time to take you to the station before I come back and ask someone else."

"It's not worth it," the other woman said under her breath to her companion. "Just tell him."

Five minutes later, Matteo was hammering on the door of a shack that looked more like an abandoned garden shed than a residence.

The door opened and a young woman stood there, gripping her robe closed at her throat. She was blonde but bleached. Her skin color was sallow. Her eyes were dull as she regarded him.

"Marie Dionne?" Matteo said.

"Yes."

He opened his notepad. "Is this your residence?"

She didn't answer and he sighed.

Why couldn't people just answer the questions and let him get on with things? At this rate it would be past lunch time before he got out of this cesspool of a slum.

"My residence," she said as if trying the word on for size.

It occurred to Matteo that she might be stoned.

"You were seen at the Chabanel harvest festival," he said slowly. "Why were you there?"

She licked her lips and then wiped them with her other hand. It was then that Matteo saw that her right hand was withered. The skin was puckered and discolored.

"I got lost," she said. "I was only there for a moment."

Matteo snapped his notebook shut and turned away, not bothering to thank her for her compliance.

Her hand was badly damaged. She couldn't have killed anyone.

This trip was a waste of time.

Plus it was probably going to rain on him on the way back to the village.

Luc noticed the clouds had darkened overhead. The afternoon had only afforded a thin dappling of sunlight and now he was about to lose that too.

After their less than successful interview with Deschamps, he'd sent Matteo to talk to the prostitute Marie Dionne who was seen at the festival and to the people who seemed to have heard Deroy accuse Jules of threatening him. Luc was on his way to talk with Jean-Joseph Dimon, Katrine Pelletier's new boyfriend.

Luc knew that Katrine and Jules were not presently

speaking to each other but he also knew that he couldn't behave in any way on this case that might suggest an impartiality. Only a few months ago, Katrine had been a regular fixture at *La Fleurette* and Luc had gotten to know her well. He missed her friendly and playful manner and knew for a fact that Jules did too.

Why couldn't women just handle their differences sensibly like men? A quick jab to the nose and a drink afterwards and then everybody goes on as if nothing had happened.

He needed to speak to Dimon mainly because he was a newcomer to the village and because Matteo had spotted him having words with Deroy. Unlike with Deschamps, that exchange hadn't turned physical.

That anyone knew.

What was the argument about?

Like so many buildings in Chabanel these days, Dimon's apartment building was largely vacant. Dating back to the eighteenth century, it must have been a showstopper in its day with its crudely carved figures of naked male torsos flanking an enormous wooden entrance. It was likely even a single residence although Luc tried to imagine what village luminary would have merited such an impressive residence.

He used his master key to open the main door since after the EMP, the electronic keypads of apartment buildings no longer worked. Once inside, he scanned the list of names over the mailboxes. Many of the boxes were nameless. Since the original owners of most apartment buildings in Chabanel were no longer around to insist on rent, Chabanel had become a village of squatters.

From the Intel Madame Gabin had collected from Marie Fournier at the *boulangerie*, Luc knew that Dimon was living in an abandoned apartment on the first floor of the building. Luc climbed the broad spiral steps to the first apartment and knocked on the door.

It took a few moments for the door to swing open revealing Jean-Joseph Dimer, a short man, balding, with a thin, sharp-boned face and shrewd grey eyes. As he stood in the doorway and recognized Luc, his expression of surprise quickly changed to agitation and annoyance.

Or possibly guilt?

"Yes?" Dimer said, blocking the doorway in case Luc decided he wanted to enter.

Luc withstood a wave of vexation. "I am Chief DeBray of the—"

"I know who you are."

"Who is it, *chérie*?" Katrine's voice came from inside.

Dimer turned his head to respond. "The police." He looked back at Luc. "I did not know the man. I exchanged no words with him."

Well, you wouldn't necessarily have to, Luc thought, *in order to kill him.*

"My Lieutenant witnessed an interaction between you and Monsieur Deroy," Luc said.

Dimer flushed and perspiration popped up on his upper lip.

"Yes, all right, I might have spoken to him now that you mention it. But it was nothing."

"My Lieutenant said it looked like an argument."

"Your man is wrong. The guy asked me for directions…to the *charcuterie* tent. That is all."

Luc knew he was lying. Matteo had said it was an argument, which hardly made sense if he was only asking for directions.

"You are new to Chabanel, Monsieur Dimer?" Luc said

as he watched Katrine emerge from the depths of the apartment and stand behind Dimer.

Luc nodded at her. "*Bonjour*, Katrine."

"Jean-Joseph didn't know the man," Katrine said, her face blushing either from lying or because she was ashamed at having been caught in Dimer's apartment. "And besides that, he was with me every second of the festival." She set her mouth in a stubborn line.

"I was asking Monsieur Dimer how it is he finds himself in Chabanel," Luc said.

"I came looking for work," Dimer said, his thin face clenching in anger that simmered just below the surface.

"Just because he's new to the village doesn't mean he killed that man!" Katrine said. "First Jules and now Jean-Joseph! You police need to find the real killer before we're all murdered in our beds!"

Well, at least she assumes that Jules isn't the real killer, Luc thought. *That's a step forward.*

"I regret that," Luc said. "But unfortunately it is my duty to talk with everyone who was at the festival yesterday and was known of have some interaction with the victim. This is not the only visit I will make today."

"Have you released Jules?" Katrine asked. "I couldn't believe Eloise did that. How upsetting that must have been for *les soeurs*."

"She has been released," Luc said before turning his attention back to Dimer. "There was much wine to enjoy at the festival. A witness might be found to say they saw you answering the call of nature at one point. *Without* Madame Pelletier."

Dimer blushed to his roots. "So go find this witness and then arrest me for taking a piss in a field!"

Even if Jules and Katrine mended their breach, Luc could not imagine under what circumstance he was ever going to be socializing with this unpleasant lout.

"Well, thank you for your time, Monsieur Dimer," Luc said. He nodded at Katrine and turned away.

While Dimer might be found to have been on his own long enough to have done the deed the fact remained that he had no obvious motive for murdering Deroy.

"Why don't you talk to Theo Bardot?" Katrine called out before Luc reached the foyer of the apartment building.

Luc turned and regarded her.

"I heard that Deroy went to him for a job and Theo threw him out in the street," she said.

"Where did you hear this?"

"Just around," Katrine said, not looking at him now. "You can ask Theo. Except he'll probably lie."

Luc knew of course that Katrine and Theo used to be friends—perhaps even more than friends. Something had happened between them and the friendship had suffered further during their acrimonious competition in the mayoral race last summer.

Luc and Matteo had already ruled Theo out as a possible suspect since Theo had gotten drunk early and passed out under the wine table. Matteo had confirmed that Theo was rarely out of his sight and for those few moments when he was, as soon as Matteo returned, he found Theo in the exact same position he'd been in when Matteo had left —curled up under the table and snoring.

Theo had been in no condition to covertly attack and kill a man and then sneak back under a table and pretend to be asleep.

Luc could more easily believe that one of *les soeurs* had

done the deed before he'd believe Theo could have managed it.

"Thank you," he said to Katrine. "I'll definitely check into it."

20

SPINNING WHEEL GOT TO GO 'ROUND

Jean-Joseph closed the door and took Katrine into his arms.

"Thank you, *chérie*. I need nothing more than my little tigress by my side defending me."

He leaned in to kiss her but Katrine pulled away.

"I was just telling the truth," she said, her stomach hardening.

She walked to the sofa and sat down where she had been before Luc interrupted them. She was sure that for all his blustering and self-righteous indignation at having to answer Luc's questions, Jean-Joseph had been relieved that their discussion had been interrupted.

Even if for an interrogation by the police.

"*Chérie*, how many times must I tell you?" Jean-Joseph said as he came back to the salon and eased himself down onto the sofa next to her. "She means nothing to me. Less than nothing. You completely misunderstood what you saw."

Katrine looked at him and saw earnest contrition in his

eyes. He took the hand she held fisted in her lap and brought it to his lips.

"Please, *chérie*," he whispered. "If you truly care for me you will believe me."

Katrine wanted very much to believe Jean-Joseph. He was the first man in her life—even before Gaultier and certainly since—who'd treated her with a sliver of decency.

Unfortunately, the fact that she had seen him at the festival with his hand up the blouse of Gigi Loumair hadn't done much to allow her to continue to maintain that fiction.

"Tell me again what happened," she said, and instantly saw the glint of victory in his eyes. He knew he'd convinced her. Or if not entirely, he knew in the end his indiscretion wouldn't matter.

Why didn't it matter? Katrine thought as she allowed him to lean her back on the couch to nuzzle her neck. Shouldn't it matter?

But then Jean-Joseph was making other arguments—less verbal arguments—for why she shouldn't think so.

21

TOOTH AND NAIL

For a change I saw Luc *before* his presence was announced to me by Cocoa's happy barking. I was in the front drive cleaning up after Roulette's many healthy deposits where the cart had been parked. I didn't have to go far with the shovel since we had a dramatic array of blood-red climbing roses flanking the front door that *les soeurs* insisted needed the fertilizer.

Since the smell of horse poo totally overpowered the fragrance of the roses I tended to think the result was a less than pleasant greeting for any guests who came to our front door. But as usual around here I was over-ruled.

I watched Luc park his car off the road so as not to come onto the gravel drive. With so few cars operating these days—as in none—he didn't have to worry about it getting hit by another vehicle so I imagine he did it to keep the oil drips to a minimum on the *La Fleurette* driveway.

I'm not sure if I've mentioned the fact that technically this *mas* belongs to Luc. Well, now that I think about it I'm not sure that's even true. But for whatever reason—and he's never divulged the reason—Luc has possession of this place.

When I was unceremoniously flung out of the apartment I'd rented as a holiday rental from Atlanta and it became clear that Léa and Justine and I wanted to live together, Luc made *La Fleurette* available to us.

As I walked toward the end of the driveway I couldn't help but think, *the joke's on him if he thinks he's ever getting this place back from Léa and Justine.*

While I believe that most people believe that when you die you can't take it with you—in the case of Léa Cazaly, I have no doubt that when *she* dies this farmhouse and all its grounds are somehow going to end up in the great beyond with her.

In any case, Luc's not ever getting it back.

I waved to him as he made his way up the gravel drive, his boots making a solid crunching sound as he walked. He was wearing a jacket because it was cool this afternoon even though the sun had warmed things up a bit. He had a dark patterned scarf knotted at his throat the way the French men do over here that always looks so odd to me—but also so sexy.

He was grinning at me in that way he does which turns my stomach upside down. I'm not sure he even knows he has this effect on me.

"Hey, you," I said as he approached. I was wearing jeans, water-repellent work boots and gloves.

"And hey to you, too," he said in his delightfully fractured English. Without missing a step, both his hands went to my waist and he drew me in close before he kissed me.

The kiss was amazing, as every kiss with Luc was—honestly I saw mini fireworks, I kid you not—and they'd been too long in coming as far as I was concerned.

"Mmmm," I murmured into his collar as he held me. "Finally."

"I missed you, *chérie*," he said, his right hand cupping my bottom in spite of the fact that *les soeurs* were likely watching from the salon window.

"Me, too," I said. "How's the case coming?"

He sighed and dropped his hand.

"Well, you can hardly not expect me to be interested," I said, "since I was your first suspect."

"You never were."

"Well, it sure felt that way when I was singing the Folsom Prison Blues down at your jailhouse."

"That was a mistake as you well know."

"Do you want to come in? I think Justine made a fresh batch of *éclairs*."

Luc shook his head and then frowned, his eyes caught on a figure materializing from the side of the house. Marco had been in the back garden raking the pathway. He approached now with Cocoa and Twig at his side. Both dogs raced to Luc in order to transfer what mud they could from their paws to Luc's clean pants.

"*Bonjour*, Chief," Marco said. "You have news?"

Luc greeted both dogs and firmly rerouted their attentions by tossing a stick, the bait for which Twig took but Cocoa didn't. Cocoa is truly the best-behaved dog in the world and she adores Luc. She settled at his feet and looked up adoringly at him.

I've felt like doing the same thing many a time.

"Not really," Luc said to Marco, his voice tense.

I snapped my attention back to him. Much of the ease and buoyancy had gone instantly out of Luc and I had to assume the arrival of Marco was the reason. In the last several months Luc has made peace with the idea of Marco —at least on some level. But the fact that Marco lives here at *La Fleurette* and is legally married to me—well, both of those facts tend to have my normally balanced and secure boyfriend in green-eyed hyper mode.

Initially I was flattered by Luc's jealousy, but now I tend to find his chronic reaction to Marco just exasperating.

"No arrests?" Marco asked. His eyes flickered to me and I realized this was Marco's subtle way of chiding Luc for allowing me to be jailed in the first place—as if Luc had had anything to do with it!

"Not yet," Luc said coolly.

"Are you sure you can't stay?" I said and threaded my arm around his waist. This was Marco's cue to go busy himself with the rake which he did but only as far as the end of the driveway. Twig came back with a different stick in his mouth and Marco wrestled it away from him and threw it again.

"Did you talk to the farmer?" I asked Luc. "The one who got in a fight with Deroy?"

"He has an alibi."

He kissed me then—quite perfunctorily I thought—and I cursed Marco's timing for breaking the spell between me and Luc—and then he turned to walk back to his car.

"Are you sure you can't come to dinner tonight?" I asked, hurrying beside him and not loving the desperate intonation in my voice.

He *always* came to dinner, although granted it was a lot less tension-filled when Marco wasn't there.

"I can't. There's an investigator coming in from Nice who I need to debrief with."

A shiver of apprehension shot through me.

"I heard about that. Is it going to look bad for you that they won't let you lead your own investigation?"

Luc's face was pinched and he jerked his chin as if his shirt-collar was suddenly too tight.

"Why did you bring him to *La Fleurette* in the first place?" he blurted out.

At first I thought he was talking about Marco who was still raking gravel but could easily hear everything we were saying from where he stood.

I felt my back stiffen. "Deroy, you mean? I thought we already covered this."

I knew Luc was annoyed but I didn't appreciate having my perfectly reasonable actions called into question. Regardless of how badly it had all worked out I hadn't done anything that might have set the stage for René Deroy getting killed. All I'd done is what any decent person would have done with an injured man down on his luck.

Now true, Deroy hadn't been injured. I'd been suckered. So maybe what Luc was really asking was w*hy were you so stupid?* And if *that was* the case, well that just made me even madder.

"Your overconfidence has gotten you into trouble again," he said to me—although his eyes were on Marco as he spoke.

I stopped walking then since it was clear there was going to be no tender goodbye kiss.

"Well, since I don't believe I did get myself into trouble, I don't see how you can call me overconfident. Which, for the record, I don't think is a bad thing!"

His back rigid, Luc lifted a hand in farewell that could just as easily have had a rude finger gesture attached to it. In fact, a part of me actually imagined I saw it even though of course it never happened.

In any case, rather than stand and watch him drive off in a huff I turned and stalked back to the house.

Marco watched the taillights on Luc's car as they disappeared down the road heading back to the village. He hated to hear Luc and Jules quarrel. Not that they did it that often.

Well, at least not that much anymore.

He could tell Luc was frustrated with not being able to protect Jules from what was happening with the murder case.

As well he should be, Marco thought in growing indignation. *Luc is her boyfriend.*

Marco regretted that he himself wasn't in a position to help Jules. But what could *he* do? He had no access to Luc's information on the case. And he certainly couldn't ask people questions. They would laugh him off their doorsteps.

That was the chief of police's job!

Marco raked at the gravel a few more minutes before he realized there was something he couldn't put his finger on buzzing around the edges of his mind.

He stopped raking and tried to think what it could be. Then he remembered *les soeurs* talking about the prostitute this morning. They seemed to think it was unusual—even suspicious—that she had been at the fair.

Could that be something?

He looked at the roofline of *La Fleurette* as an idea began to form in his mind.

Jules can't go to the Mégisseries, where the prostitute lives. It is way too dangerous.

But I can.

22
TESTING THE WATERS

Eloise gnawed on a ragged fingernail and sat in the corner of the Chief's office. Dobry had left to go find a late lunch in the village but Eloise hadn't felt comfortable leaving with him. Madame Gabin was back at her post at the front desk and Eloise didn't want Dobry knowing the Chief had suspended her—and Madame G would have immediately informed him if she'd laid eyes on Eloise.

Eloise hated hiding out in the Chief's office. What if he returned before Dobry did? She'd have to explain why she was in uniform and why she was there.

Perhaps she should have gone with Dobry after all? He was a funny sort. All business but also just informal enough to let Eloise know he wasn't happy being dragged to Chabanel for this case. Or had she imagined that?

After everything that had happened, she didn't know what to think any more. First, Marco was head over heels in love and talking about getting married and then all of a sudden, *poof!* he wanted to "take a break."

She felt her body tense. There was no doubt that Jules Hooker was behind *that* idea.

And after I nearly lost my job doing her that favor last summer!

Eloise went to the window and looked out. Luc still wasn't back yet and neither was Matteo although Matteo wouldn't care what Eloise did. She could hear Madame G moving about in the front of the station.

How did this happen? How did it happen that I am sneaking around my own place of work? As hard as I have worked for the last five years! And all it took was one American woman who shouldn't be here in the first place and my whole career is in jeopardy.

Not to mention the love of my life.

Just thinking about Marco and how he avoided her now made Eloise want to weep. She turned to see from the Chief's window if she could catch a glimpse of him at the café.

Marco used to be so happy to see her. His whole face used to light up at the thought of spending the evening with her. How did it all go wrong? How could he turn from her now?

But she knew how.

Because of Jules.

From the window Eloise saw Dobry emerge from the terrace of Café Sucre and walk across the square toward the police station. He was a tall man but his shoulders slumped forward in an unattractive way. As he walked, he reached down and scratched his crotch without a care in the world that anyone might be watching.

Eloise made a face and pulled back before he saw her.

Why was he still here at the office? Shouldn't he go out to *La Fleurette* and drag Jules down to the station?

The whole point of him coming was to do what Luc wouldn't do!

Clearly, Eloise needed to be more direct with him.

She sat down in the chair opposite the desk and waited for Dobry to enter the office.

"You are still here?" he said with surprise as he entered the office.

Fighting back her irritation at his comment, Eloise smiled at him.

"I thought you might need my assistance," she said. "I am very familiar with the case and can brief you in detail."

"I think you've told me everything, have you not?" he said, patting his jacket pockets and pulling out a packet of cigarettes. "The victim had a physical altercation with a hothead farmer moments before he was found dead." He shrugged and lit the cigarette. "That's our lead right there."

Eloise looked at him, dumbfounded. He was looking at the *farmer* for this?

"But...but Jules Hooker admitted to threatening the victim. And it was *her* weapon that was used on him."

He made a face. "But she is a woman."

Eloise took in a long breath to keep her voice steady.

"A very capable woman. The lipstick on the victim's mouth shows that—"

"Eh? Did you mention lipstick before?" He looked down at the case folder on the desk and flipped through it. "Yes, I see."

"So that shows he had recent contact with a woman and Jules Hooker wears lipstick."

"But if she was overheard threatening him, is it likely she would be kissing him?"

Eloise pinched her lips together. "She might if she wanted to get close enough to cut his throat."

"Pretty cold blooded I would have thought. This American isn't a professional assassin, is she?" He grinned at his joke. "No, I will question the farmer first. What's his name? Deschamps?" He looked at the file again. "I will speak to him immediately."

"I believe the Chief and Lieutenant Matteo were speaking with him this morning," Eloise said between gritted teeth. "They will have their notes when they return today."

Dobry sat back down and flicked his cigarette ash on the floor.

"Well, then I'll wait for them to return," he said.

Her insides churning with uncertainty and doubt, Eloise watched him smoke for a moment before making a decision about her next move. Seeing that his focus was on the end of his cigarette and not her, she surreptitiously unbuttoned the top three buttons of her uniform blouse and pushed her breasts out to strain against the material.

If this idiot thinks a woman is less likely to murder than a man then he'll certainly be receptive to a few other stereotypes.

Stereotypes I can use.

"Detective?" she said as she leaned over the desk, making sure her cleavage was on full display, and pointed to a paragraph in the file.

Dobry cleared his throat and sat up straight, alerting her without needing to see for herself that he was responding to her ploy.

She tapped a sheet in the file folder. "If you look right here you'll see that Jules Hooker has not even been interviewed yet."

Dobry cleared his throat again and Eloise felt a surge of power at his reaction to her. She had never in her life done anything remotely like what she was doing now.

Frankly, she never thought she had the attributes to do it.

Turned out she was wrong about that.

"And while I know Chief DeBray will tell you he *did* take her statement," Eloise purred, "I'm sure whatever interrogation she received at his hands was not pointed in the direction of trying to find a murderer."

"Yes. I see," Dobry said, glancing up from the file folder to Eloise's bulging blouse.

"So I was really hoping that you, Detective, would be able to re-interview Jules Hooker who as I've mentioned has motive, opportunity, means but no alibi."

"I see," Dobry said again, looking up at Eloise's eyes.

Oh, Marco, the things I do for you.

"I mean, she *did* discover the body and it *was* her murder weapon," Eloise said, pursing her lips to make them look as pouty as possible.

"That is a good point."

"And she did threaten to kill him that very morning. Several people will testify to that."

He leaned over the desk toward her. "That is very damning indeed," he said, licking his lips. "Now that I think about it, I believe I must concur that Jules Hooker is clearly the prime suspect in this case."

Eloise felt a flush of warmth radiate throughout her body. She put one hip on the desk and edged her way over toward him, her lips ever closer to his face.

"Shall I see that she is brought to Grighot immediately? In case she tries to run?"

"I think that is an excellent suggestion," he said hoarsely.

23

EVERY LITTLE THING SHE DOES

Theo twisted in the stone alcove of the alley where he sat observing the apartment door. He'd been there since he witnessed Katrine enter the building four hours earlier. He had been sure at the time that she wouldn't stay long. After all she had children who needed minding.

The tight space was uncomfortable and as he waited he continually had to stretch his legs to alleviate the cramping that shot up his thighs.

By the second hour he'd already drained the flask of cognac but felt no better for it. He wanted another drink but even greater than his need for more alcohol was his desire to see Katrine when she left the man's apartment.

He'd watched Chief DeBray an hour earlier hesitate in front of the big door and then enter the building only to return less than a quarter of an hour later.

Had DeBray talked to Katrine's man? Had Katrine defended him? Alibied him? Had the Chief caught them *in flagrante*?

Theo's breathing was coming in short, hard pants now.

Had Katrine come to the door barefoot, a robe falling off her barely-concealed nude body? Before or *after* she'd laid with that bastard?

Theo literally saw spots before his eyes as he clenched his jaw.

Whore! Who was watching her children?

Theo had thought Katrine was a good mother until now. Now he knew she was exactly as he'd assessed her months ago. A woman with no morals and no decency.

DeBray had left over an hour ago. Why was Katrine still inside? Were they talking about the Chief's visit?

Were they laughing at me?

Theo knew he'd made a spectacle of himself at the festival. He'd been assured of that by no fewer than five busybodies from the village. He'd hung his head at each admonishment.

Would they be astonished to know that it had all been an act?

Well, not all of it. He'd been drunk enough, God knows.

He'd had to be in order to do what he needed to do.

How could Katrine be so oblivious? How could she not know he'd done it all for her?

Suddenly the door to the apartment building opened and reflexively, Theo drew his legs in, his body tense and ready.

Katrine stepped out into the street, hesitating on the doorstep and then looked both ways down the narrow cobblestone lane.

Like a common whore. Brazenly servicing the man upstairs but ashamed for her neighbors to see who she really was.

Theo felt a rush of malevolence and urgency and without further thought pushed himself to his feet and stepped out of his hiding place.

Katrine had her back to him, her thoughts clearly focused on escape and her tryst and not the soft thuds of footfalls behind her.

Theo waited until she was almost at the cross street where there were sure to be people. He felt a quickening of his pulse at the thought that his chance would then be lost.

"Katrine!"

She turned, looking at him over her shoulder. Her eyes were wide with recognition and shame. She quickened her pace.

In four long strides, he caught up to her. He grabbed her arm and twisted her around harshly. She shrieked and went down on one knee on the cobblestones, a hand against his leg to steady herself.

He didn't remember what he'd intended to tell her because somewhere in the deep cognac-soaked recesses of his brain he knew he'd had a plan. But now, looking at her terrified face as she looked up at him, a scream clearly clawing up her throat, all he could think of was that she had lain with a stranger just minutes ago.

He could smell the man on her.

"I know what you did," Theo growled, his fingers tightening on her arm as he wrenched her to her feet.

"Theo, please no," she said, her lips and chin trembling.

"*Theo, please, no,*" he mocked her. "Is that what you told *him*? Did you tell *him* no?" He flung her from him, disgusted with her. With himself.

Because she'd never listen to him now.

The sounds of people talking came to both of them. They were close to the main street of the village. He could see by the expression on her face that she heard them too.

Before he could change tactics, before he could explain, she swiveled on one foot and darted down the street, disappearing around the corner where Theo knew the village market would be in the process of breaking down.

He didn't bother running after her.

She'd escaped him again.

For now.

24

THE SHORT END

Marco had been to the *Mégisseries* before.
He'd gone with Thibault once to pick up a load of plumbing pieces from an abandoned building and then later he returned to find a girl. He blushed at the memory.

Everyone thought he was so good-looking. Even the whores laughed at the thought that he might need to pay for sex. But he was lonely.

That was before Eloise of course. After he was with her he hadn't needed to return to the *Mégisseries*.

The *Mégisseries* was a slum and he should know. He'd lived in enough of them in his short life. The street he walked down was quiet but he could feel the eyes watching him.

Although he didn't know Marie Dionne by sight he knew he didn't need to. If he was lucky he might not even have to talk with the prostitute herself. He prayed that *she* hadn't been the one all those months ago for that night in the *Mégisseries*. His ears burned again at the memory.

But Marie *had* been at the festival the day Deroy was

murdered. And *les soeurs* seemed to think that was unusual. That was enough for Marco.

If the Chief wasn't going to do his job to clear Jules of this crime then Marco would have to do it. After all, he *was* her husband.

He didn't fool himself into thinking his relationship with Jules was anything more than it was. They were legally married, true, but they were friends. He didn't wish for more than that but he still believed—married or not—that it was his responsibility to help her when she was in trouble.

It should be the Chief doing it but the important thing was that it got done.

"Help you, *chérie*?" a voice called out as he passed. "Got something to pay me with?"

She was hawk-faced and looked at least fifty. But she was dressed to make no doubt about her profession.

"I have some money," Marco said.

The woman laughed, revealing two missing teeth. "Where would I spend money?"

Marco reached into his pocket and drew out the half chocolate bar he'd stolen from the kitchen at *La Fleurette*. He watched the woman's eyes widen.

"Is that real?" she asked.

"It's real," he said holding it out to her. "Black market dark chocolate."

She slipped into place beside him, her arm on his arm, her eyes on the chocolate bar.

"What will you have, Monsieur? I used to be a gymnast."

At first Marco thought she was making a joke and he blushed again when he realized she was serious.

"I need information about a friend of yours," he said.

The woman frowned and Marco felt her hands tighten

around his arm. She was not about to let the chocolate get away.

"I have many friends," she said, licking her lips. "What do you want to know?"

Twenty minutes later Marco stood on the threshold of a wooden shack at the very edge of the *Mégisseries*. Unlike the other structures which were shared by groups or even whole families, this shed was small and dark with no hint that someone lived within.

He knocked on the door.

"I am not working today!" a high-pitched voice called out.

"I am looking for Marie Dionne," Marco said, keeping the image of Jules in his head and forcing himself not to turn around and go home.

He could hear sounds from inside and within a moment the door opened a crack. A woman glared at him.

"What do you want?" Marie asked.

She wasn't homely, which surprised Marco. He thought all whores were either old or ugly. Or else why did they become prostitutes?

"My name is Marco Alaoui. May I talk to you, Mademoiselle Dionne?"

"You are police? Again?"

That surprised Marco. He assumed the police wouldn't bother talking to the prostitute. Maybe this was a wasted trip after all?

"I am here for a friend," Marco said, not knowing what else to say. "I need your help."

Marco was used to his good looks opening doors for him and today proved no exception. Literally. Marie pretended to be aloof but he could tell by the way she pushed the door open before she turned away that she was interested in hearing what he wanted.

And he was pretty sure she wouldn't have done that if he looked like Detective Adrien Matteo.

He followed her inside and glanced around. The room was as rude and filthy as he'd imagined from the outside but she'd done what she could to make it comfortable. A flowered duvet was bunched on the narrow bed that was front and center in the room. He grimaced at the sight of the bed and felt even more disconcerted.

Marie stood next to the bed. She held her elbows and regarded him shrewdly.

Marco struggled to think what the best approach would be. After what the first whore had told him, he had every reason to think Marie might incriminate herself if he just presented it right.

Presenting things right was not Marco's strong suit. Not when the things were words or ideas.

She was already wary of him. It was only natural that she would resist telling him anything bad about herself—regardless of how much it would help Jules. Plus, Marie had already talked to the police. The fact that she was not in jail meant they'd got nothing useful from her.

He sighed. He had no idea of how to go forward. As usual, the only ace he had in his hand was his good looks and from the way she was eyeing him, he could tell she was thinking the same thing.

Not for the first time in his life, Marco accepted the hand he'd been dealt and proceeded to play it.

He sat down on her bed and picked up her hand not realizing until he touched it that the hand was not right.

Forcing himself not to recoil he held it firmly and caressed it with his thumb.

"Who did this to you, *chérie*?"

He had no idea that she hadn't been born with it. But he did know it was important for her to think he cared. Actually, he did care. It broke his heart to see this lovely creature brought to this. She could be his own sister. Or his mother.

He lifted his eyes to hers and was shocked to realize that beyond the surprise and the fear he saw in her face was a desperate need to believe that Marco was not repelled by her.

"The man who lies dead in the vineyard forest," Marie said softly, sinking to the bed next to Marco.

Marco's mouth fell open and within seconds he realized the truth.

If Deroy mutilated this girl then she had every reason to want him dead.

He tried to hide the sudden lightness he felt in his chest.

"You knew Deroy?" he asked, willing Marie to speak to him, to trust him.

Her eyes filled with angry tears.

"René was my brother," she said bitterly. She looked at Marco's shocked face and then held her withered hand up between them. "And this was the least of what that monster did to me."

As Marco struggled to make sense of what she was telling him, Marie gripped his hand and continued as if she'd been waiting all along to tell someone her story.

"He came to me the day before the festival demanding money. When I refused, he threatened me with blackmail. I told him I'd kill him before I gave anything more to him."

Marco wasn't sure what exactly she was saying beyond that she was Deroy's sister and that she threatened to kill him but one thing was for sure—he was fairly positive Marie hadn't told *this* to Detective Matteo.

Would it be enough?

Would it be enough to get them to stop looking at Jules?

"Is that why he came to Chabanel?" Marco asked. "To see you?"

Marie snorted and dropped her hand into her lap.

"Not just me. He came to talk to the poor stupid girl he married all those years ago."

Marco's ears pricked up. "He has a wife in Chabanel?"

She shook her head. "*Had* a wife. Her father had the marriage annulled a long time since."

Was this important information? Marco frowned. Did it matter now that the man was dead? Marco felt eager to get back to *La Fleurette* and tell Jules what he'd found out. Jules would know how to make sense of it all.

He stood up. He could hear that a gentle rain had begun outside.

"You are leaving?" Marie said, her shoulders slumping. "Do you have to? Can't you stay?"

"I cannot," he said, about to pat her shoulder and then realizing he didn't have the stomach to touch her again.

"Will you come back?" she asked, following him to the door. "I could tell you more things. Don't you want to know who René married?"

Marco made it through the door before turning and smiling at Marie.

"Yes?" he said, already anticipating how wet he was going to get on his jog back to *La Fleurette* and hoping the twins had made soup for lunch. "Who was it he married?"

"You won't believe when I tell you," Marie said, following him out onto the porch and into the rain. "Nobody would."

"Oh? Why is that?" Marco said pleasantly, not wanting to be rude but really wanting to be on his way. His stomach rumbled in anticipation of the soup.

"Because she's a Detective Sergeant, that's why," Marie said.

Marco stopped in his half turn to leave the porch and felt the drill of the icy rain find its way down his collar. He stared at her.

"What did you say?"

"René's first wife," Marie said, clearly delighted to have recaptured Marco's attention. "It was Eloise Basile."

25

TIME'S UP

The evening air felt thick with rain that should have fallen today but hadn't.

Or maybe it was just the feeling of the shoe that hadn't dropped yet.

Luc rolled his neck before he got out of the car in front of the police station. It had been a long day, made longer by his ill-advised stop at *La Fleurette* where he had behaved like an ass. He felt a flush of remorse remembering how he'd bickered with Jules just when he'd meant to be supportive and reassuring with her.

And all because I can't stop reacting to a man who I have no earthly reason to feel threatened by.

Luc climbed out of his car and spotted Adrien Matteo walking across the village square toward him. Even Matteo walked as if he had a fifty-kilo weight on his shoulders. Luc could tell at a glance that the detective hadn't discovered anything helpful in his day's worth of canvassing either.

They met at the foot of the stairs leading to the *police municipale*.

"Anything?" Luc asked, knowing the answer.

Matteo shook his head. "I'm hoping the lab results are back."

For all the good that will do, Luc couldn't help but think. Even if the lab report showed Jules' prints were on the knife —if it was *her* knife, that would simply make sense. The notebook found in Deroy's backpack had only a few scribbled notes in it with no dates. And the other more incriminating item—found beneath Deroy's body—well, there could be a million reasons for that.

"Chief?" Matteo said, frowning as he stood beside the motorbike parked in front of the stairs.

"The independent investigator from HQ," Luc said, with a heavy sigh. "Might as well see what he has to say."

The two entered the station and Madame Gabin immediately got to her feet from behind her receptionist's desk.

"Chief," she said. "You have a visitor in your office."

"Is the lab report in yet?" he asked as he turned toward his office. It would've helped immensely if he and Matteo had found something in their day of statement-gathering to help direct them. He'd been hoping they'd find something to lay on the table that didn't have Jules Hooker's name written all over it.

Madame Gabin handed a sheet of paper to Matteo who scanned it briefly.

"Anything?" Luc asked.

"No prints on the knife," Matteo said grimly.

Which meant it had been wiped.

Luc paused outside his office door. "And the notebook?"

Matteo shook his head. "Just Deroy's prints."

Dragging his footsteps and fighting off discouragement, Luc opened the door to this office.

Eloise jumped to her feet from where she'd been

lounging across his desk and turned her back. Luc could have sworn she was buttoning her blouse.

Before he even glanced at the man sitting in his desk chair, Luc felt an irrational fury beginning to build.

"What's going on here?" he demanded.

The man stood up and held out his hand. "Detective Lieutenant Marc Dobry," he said.

Luc shook hands with him. "What can I help you with, Detective Dobry?"

Dobry snatched up a folded sheet of paper from the desk top and presented it to Luc.

"I'm actually here to help you, Chief," Dobry said.

Luc took the paper and moved to the side of the desk, prompting Dobry to scurry from around it to stand next to Eloise who was looking decidedly flushed.

"You sick?" Matteo asked her in a low voice.

"Shut up," Eloise hissed at him, her hands still straightening her uniform blouse.

Luc scanned the papers and tossed them on the desk.

"I'm sorry you had to drive all the way from Nice," he said. "We have the investigation under control."

"With all due respect, Chief," Dobry said evenly, "that is not my assessment."

Luc watched Dobry glance at Eloise who had the shame at least to blush.

"While I'm very interested to hear the results of your and Lieutenant Matteo's day of canvassing," Dobry said, crossing his arms and rocking back on his heels, "I have to say I'm surprised to hear you no longer have your prime suspect in custody."

Luc refused to glance at Eloise. Clearly he'd underestimated her. That she would be willing to not only go over his head to HQ but to defy a direct order told him she was a lot further gone than he'd realized.

Eloise stared at the carpeted floor, her cheeks flaming.

Before Luc could respond to Dobry's comment, Dobry turned to Matteo.

"I'll need you to bring in Jules Hooker so that I may question her," Dobry said.

"No one is bringing anyone in," Luc said. "We don't have the evidence yet to make an arrest and I'm not jumping the gun until we do."

"So it's true," Dobry said, turning back to Luc. "You are biased. I will need to put this in my report."

"I don't care *where* you put it," Luc said flexing his fists at his sides. "This is my district, my case."

"Lieutenant Dobry has a right to question the suspect," Eloise said, her voice tremulous as she finally looked at Luc.

"Go home, Sergeant," Luc said. "I'll deal with you later."

"Sergeant Basile is instrumental to this investigation," Dobry said. "I must insist she remain."

A part of Luc wanted to laugh out loud. What the hell had these two gotten up to in here? Eloise looked nervous but defiant, her eyes red-rimmed as if she'd been crying or was about to.

Bottom line, his sergeant was falling apart.

"If I have to ask you again, Sergeant," Luc said, "I'll take your badge."

"You can't do that!" Eloise said, looking at Dobry as if to confirm that Luc couldn't. Then she sucked in a breath and faced Luc. "After the detective questions her, Jules Hooker is being taken immediately to Grighot."

Luc snorted in disgust but felt his pulse speed up in mounting fury.

"Sergeant Basile is correct," Dobry said. "We'll need to

detain Jules Hooker in order to prevent her from fleeing until we can uncover all the evidence."

"You mean you'll detain her *without* arresting her?" Matteo said with a frown. "Is that legal?"

"No, it's not," Luc said. "So it won't be happening."

"I think you'll find it *will* happen, Chief," Dobry said firmly. "Jules Hooker is not French. She has no rights in this country."

Luc saw Eloise's shoulders relax and her earlier nervousness seemed to dissipate.

"Of course she has rights," Luc said. "And I won't allow you to do it."

"Careful, Chief," Dobry said. "You already have one complaint of bias against you. I'd hate to have to give neutral testimony to confirm that complaint firsthand. If your man won't go collect her, Sergeant Basile and I will."

For one mad moment Luc's mind raced trying to imagine if there was any way he could get word to Jules to tell her to hide, to run, to...

But at that moment Luc heard a sharp knock on his office door just before it swung open and Jules entered the room.

26

CLEAN-UP ON AISLE FOUR

Ever go into a room and get the sensation that everyone was just talking about you?

Luc and Matteo were standing in Luc's office with some guy I'd never seen before but assumed must be the "impartial" investigator from Nice. And Eloise was there too. What a party!

The last time I'd seen Luc we hadn't left things very pleasantly and I had hopes that would change after I told him Marco's bombshell.

When Marco came home this afternoon and told me what he'd discovered, I'd been totally dumbfounded—for about five seconds—and then I grabbed him and headed straight for the police station to lay this juicy, er, I mean pertinent piece of information at Luc's feet.

I don't know about you but finding out that Eloise not only knew the victim but had been married to him at one point felt like a very big deal in the general scheme of things.

Talk about bias! And motive! It felt like a watershed

piece of information and I was sure Luc would see it that way too.

The minute Marco and I heard all the shouting coming from Luc's office—Eloise's voice the most prominent of all—I started to feel a little bad about what we'd come to reveal about her. For one thing as soon as I got past the thankfully empty receptionist's desk and stepped into Luc's office I could see Eloise looked like pure hell.

Her blouse was mis-buttoned and her hair was a mess and her lipstick was...hey, wait a minute! I glanced at the new guy and wouldn't you know it, he was wearing the same shade of lipstick as Eloise!

I think right about then I officially became very unsympathetic about sticking Eloise in it. After all, there was no doubt *she* was trying to nail *me* for a murder I didn't commit.

And all *I* was going to do was shatter her credibility and publicly ruin her life.

The stranger turned to me and Marco where we stood in the doorway.

"Jules Hooker, I presume?" he said, his eyes glittering.

"Stand down, Detective," Luc growled at him.

Aw, my hero.

It was nice seeing Luc so protective of me, even if his face was all twisted up in an ugly scowl. Kind of like the last time I saw him at *La Fleurette* now that I think about it.

"Detective Matteo, please put Madame Hooker in an interview room," mean-faced stranger said, never taking his eyes off me.

Matteo didn't move.

Eloise shoved past Matteo to reach me. "I'll do it!" she said.

She had one hand on me before Marco pushed her back. She rocked on her heels, catching herself on the side of the desk, her eyes blinking with shock that he'd been so rough with her.

"No one is touching her," Marco said. "We have come with information that will change everything!"

"How dare you touch an officer of the law!" Eloise shrieked.

"Sergeant Basile," Luc said, "go home right this minute or I'll put you in one of the cells. That is an order!"

"You saw what he did!" Eloise said, looking at Dobry and then Matteo and Luc, her eyes wide with affront. "He attacked me!"

I thought it was about time to end all this nonsense.

"Marco went to the *Mégisseries* today," I said to Luc, "and talked to Marie Dionne who was at the festival."

"To what end?" Matteo said, narrowing his eyes at Marco. "I interviewed her myself today. She wasn't there long enough to do anything or talk to anyone."

"That's not what she told *me*," Marco said, his eyes on Eloise.

There must have been something about the way he looked at her because I swear I heard her whimper like she knew what was coming.

"Marie Dionne told Marco she was related to Deroy by marriage," I said. "It turns out she's Deroy's stepsister." I turned to Detective Matteo. "Did she tell you that?"

Matteo frowned and flipped open his notepad and looked at his notes. I'm pretty sure he was trying to stall for time because you either knew something like that or you didn't.

"She's *related* to Deroy?" Luc said, frowning.

Eloise backed up toward the wall. I couldn't help but notice she looked at least three shades paler.

"She told me Deroy visited her the day before the festival," Marco said. "He wanted money. When she refused, he threatened her with blackmail."

"Blackmail for what?" Dobry asked.

Marco shrugged. "She didn't say but she told him she'd rather kill him than give in to him. I talked to two people in the *Mégisseries* who said they heard her threaten to kill Deroy."

"You have names of these people?" Dobry said, glancing briefly at poor Matteo who was still studying his notes, his neck growing redder by the minute.

Marco nodded and then turned to Eloise. "And more."

"Well, let's have it, Marco," Luc said testily. I could tell by the glance he gave Detective Matteo that he was *not* at all pleased to be getting this information from *Marco* of all people instead of his own detective. I had a feeling Matteo would be hearing about it before the night was over.

"Marie said that Deroy had a friend in the village," Marco said. "A very *good* friend. So good in fact that they'd once been married to each other!"

Eloise broke down sobbing then and Luc and Dobry both turned and looked at her, their eyes widening in shock.

"Sergeant?" Luc said, looking first at Marco and then back at Eloise. "Is this true? You were *married* to René Deroy?"

Eloise crumpled to the floor, her hands covering her face as she sobbed noisily.

Dobry snorted in disgust. "What is the matter with this place? You're all lunatics!"

"Marco, I'm sorry!" Eloise wailed. "Please forgive me."

"Look," I said, deciding that Eloise had been punished enough. "I'm not sure what any of this means but I thought it was worth throwing into the mix and so that's why we're here. Luc?" I caught his eye. "I'm sorry about this afternoon.

I hope this new information is helpful. Marco and I are going back to *La Fleurette* now."

I turned and touched Marco's shoulder to indicate the show was over when I felt strong fingers pinching into my bicep where Dobry grabbed me.

"Oh, no, you don't," Dobry said, tightening his fingers on my arm. "This new information does nothing to prove that *you* did not kill Deroy. You are merely attempting to distract us from the focus of our investigation."

"You're hurting me," I said, twisting my body to get away from his punishing grasp.

"I'll do more than that if you don't come along quietly," he said. "You are still our prime suspect and we—"

What happened next was a Marco-blur that catapulted itself onto the detective which resulted in the two of them hitting and then rolling on the floor of Luc's office effectively knocking *me* down and a torchier lamp with me.

All I heard were crashes, grunts, Eloise's weeping and Luc shouting. In other words, it was chaos in the police station.

By the time I'd scrambled to my feet and gotten out of the way of the two men wrestling on the floor I could see Marco pulling his arm back in order to clock the nice police officer underneath him and I shouted, "Marco, no!" about the time Luc grabbed Marco's arm and hauled him off Dobry.

Dobry climbed to his feet, his face red, his lip bloody, his eyes absolutely crazy, but before he could say anything, Madame Gabin was in the doorway bellowing, "Quiet! Everyone!"

And you know what? Everyone shut up and turned to look at her in numb stupefaction. Madame Gabin stood there, all two hundred pounds of her, one arm wrapped around the bony shoulders of a small girl, no more than twelve years old, whose eyes were wide at the shenanigans of some seriously deranged adults in the police chief's office.

When Madame Gabin was sure she had our attention, she looked at Luc and indicated the girl with a nod of her head.

"This is Angelique Deschamps. Michel Deschamps daughter."

The air in the room changed immediately. Madame Gabin looked at Angelique and said softly, "Do you want me to tell them or do you want to?"

Angelique took in a big breath and turned to face us. She was a small girl but now that I had time to examine her face I could see she was probably more like thirteen or fourteen. Her face was thin and her dark brown hair hung limply to her shoulders.

"I came here to tell you that the real reason my father was so angry at the harvest festival was because the man who was killed...tried to...make babies with me."

27

ALL COMES TUMBLIN' DOWN

The tide of anger that swept through me at Angelique's words felt like a wildfire scouring everything in its path.

I could tell by the muscle twitching in Luc's cheek that he felt the same way. Instantly, he went to the girl and knelt in front of her. The rest of us just stared in stunned silence —even Dobry.

"Thank you for coming, Angelique," Luc said to her. "That was very brave of you."

"I had to," she said. "Papa said he was going to kill him."

Luc looked up at Madame Gabin.

"Madame Gabin, can you see if we have any hot chocolate left for our guest? And sit with her in the interview room until I can come?"

Madame Gabin nodded and patted the girl's shoulder. "Yes, Chief."

The minute Madame Gabin and the girl left the room, Luc turned to Matteo.

"Go back out to Deschamps' farm. Bring both Madame and Monsieur Deschamps in immediately."

Matteo nodded and slipped out of the room.

Shocked briefly into silence by what Angelique had said, Eloise was now back to focusing on her own very delicate situation.

"Marco, forgive me!" she said as tears streamed down her face. "I was young. I didn't know what I was doing!"

"You lied," Marco said to her. "You lied to make Jules look guilty."

Eloise covered her face with both hands, muffling the sounds of her sobs.

"Excuse me!" Dobry said as Luc went back to his desk. "I want to make a formal complaint against this hoodlum who attacked me. And I want to go on the record to say I always thought Deschamps was our main suspect." He gave Eloise a glare to punctuate his statement.

"I didn't mean it," Eloise said to Marco, going to him now and grabbing his arms. "Please, Marco. You have to believe me."

"Marie Dionne said she saw you kiss him!" Marco said in indignation.

Marco had left that part out of what he'd told me earlier.

Eloise kissed Deroy? The day he was murdered?

Eloise gasped and looked at everyone in the room in horror.

"It wasn't like that," she said, her eyes on Luc now.

"You *knew* we were looking at the lipstick as a key piece of evidence," Luc said. "You also knew that it was one more declaration against Jules for the murder. And all along, you knew it was *your* lipstick?"

"Chief! You can't think *I* killed him!" Eloise said, now looking from Marco to Luc in desperation.

"Why not?" Luc said. "If the fact of the lipstick was enough to be used against Jules, why not you?"

I could tell that Luc was furious and I could also tell he was having a hard time hiding his disgust and surprise at the shocking news that Eloise had kissed the victim.

I cleared my throat. "So *why* did you kiss him?" I asked since it looked like Luc wasn't going to.

Eloise looked at me with almost gratitude in her eyes at the opportunity to deflect from her crimes to at least explain herself.

"He kissed *me*," she said. "He grabbed me—"

"But you met with him secretly," Dobry said. "On the day of the murder. All along, you knew you'd interacted with him but you kept that to yourself."

"I...I know," she said, wiping her tears. "And that was wrong. But it wasn't important! How could it be important if I wasn't the one who killed him?"

"How do we know it wasn't you?" Marco said coldly.

"Marco, no! You have to believe me. René...grabbed me and kissed me. I ran away!"

"So you say," Marco said.

Whoa. This was a whole new Marco I was seeing. Gone was the warm and fuzzy do-anything-for-you-sweetie-pie we all knew and loved and in his place was a man who'd been lied to. He looked stone-faced and unforgiving.

"I swear it's the truth!" Eloise said. "Please, Marco. You have to believe me."

Marco snorted and turned toward me, his brown eyes sad but resolute. Whatever he'd felt for Eloise—even the pity or sadness that he'd felt when he'd ended their relationship—it was gone now.

Long gone.

"Marco," Luc said, surprising both Marco and me since Luc never addressed Marco directly. "I need you to take Jules home."

Marco nodded and without a single glance at the still-sobbing Eloise, took me firmly by the arm and led me out of the office and onto the street into the evening air.

"Pull yourself together," Luc said wearily to Eloise from where she sat huddled on the floor of his office, her shoulders shaking with her silent sobs.

"I'd say you've got your pick of suspects now, Chief," Dobry said as he fished out a cigarette pack from his jacket.

"I didn't mean to do it," Eloise said softly from where she sat on the floor.

Luc wanted to tell her to shut up before she totally incriminated herself, but that wasn't his job.

"Get out," he said wearily to Dobry. "If you read your orders you know your assistance is predicated on my acceptance of it."

Dobry lit his cigarette with a book of matches and tossed the spent match on the floor near where Eloise sat sniffling. It took all of Luc's willpower not to make the *couchon* pick it up with his teeth.

"I'm more than happy to leave this insane asylum but you may be less than pleased with the report I intend to file when I get back to HQ."

"I'm sure no one of consequence will read it," Luc said, "so file away." He glanced at his watch. He didn't want to keep little Angelique waiting and he expected Matteo back any time now with the girl's parents in tow.

Dobry sucked on his cigarette, giving Eloise a gimlet eye and turning toward the door.

"In any case you should know that in all likelihood your timeline for solving this case just tightened because my report will state that in my estimation the chief of police is incapable of being impartial on the case."

Luc sat down at his desk and picked up the case file. If the man wasn't gone in fifteen more seconds, he would very likely be forced to do something that would not look good on his permanent record.

Dobry continued to stand in the doorway.

"It's true my professional involvement in this case may have been discretionary but the complaint has been lodged and registered," Dobry said. "You'll have to arrest someone, Chief and soon, or lose your job for losing your objectivity."

He turned on his heel and disappeared out the door, saving Luc from having to act on his emotions.

Eloise climbed to her feet and sagged into a nearby chair in front of the desk.

"I'm sorry," she said in a small voice.

"I know." He handed her a tissue from his desk drawer and waited while she dried her tears and took a long, chest-rattling breath. "Tell me what happened."

"I married him when I was sixteen. It was annulled three months later and I hadn't seen him since." Eloise's face was red and puffy and she wiped her nose on her sleeve. "Just like with Marie Dionne, he came to my apartment last week asking for money. When I told him no, he threatened to blackmail me."

The diary found in Deroy's backpack had notes jotted in it that could be construed as intent to blackmail someone. The phrase "married to me" had been underlined in a recent entry and until this moment had been too cryptic to connect to the case. No longer.

"You spoke with him at the festival?"

She squeezed her eyes shut as if it was too painful to recall the incident.

"I saw him there. He got me off alone and we argued. He...he tried to kiss me. I have no idea why. I pushed him away and ran off. The next time I saw him he was dead."

Luc sighed. This whole case had effectively blown up in his face—and taken half his police force with it.

Not only that but it was clear that spending any more time with Jules during all this would only end up looking bad for her down the road—especially if it turned out God forbid that she went to trial for the murder.

For her sake he'd have to stay away until this thing got sorted out.

"Chief?" Eloise said. "Are you very angry with me?"

Luc shook off his discouraging thoughts and refocused on Eloise's tear-stained face.

"Why would Deroy's threat to reveal you were married to him be worthy of blackmail? Why would anyone care?"

Eloise gave a sad hollow laugh, her eyes miserable and bereft.

"It wasn't about the marriage," she said. "It was about something I did when I was very young. And trust me. Everyone would care."

28

DEAD TO RIGHTS

Jean-Joseph stood outside the bakery in Chabanel waiting for the teenager, Eliana. It was late and the bakery had closed an hour ago but the girl had given him a few glances this afternoon that made him believe she might be receptive to expanding their acquaintance.

He peered in the darkened window and could see the baker—the hard-nosed big shouldered lesbian—in the far back of the building where the ovens were.

Had he missed the girl? He looked around and noticed her bike was missing and he cursed the fact that he'd stayed too long with Katrine and had missed his chance with Eliana.

Jamming his hands in his pocket, he turned to walk back to his apartment when he heard voices coming from the village square. He stopped and waited until he saw the chief of police emerge from the police station.

The chief was clearly visible in the dim puddle of light the street lamps shone onto the pavement. Jean-Joseph slid into the shadows and watched the police chief turn to someone with him. Jean-Joseph realized it was the girl sergeant Eloise.

Jean-Joseph observed them until Eloise turned and walked away. The police chief watched her go and then glanced around the square as if looking for something. Jean-Joseph pulled his face back into the dark recess, his heart pounding in fear that he'd been spotted.

His interview with DeBray yesterday had done nothing to reassure him that the police weren't looking at him. It was clear that the policeman hadn't believed him when he said he'd had nothing to do with Deroy.

Katrine had insisted to the police that she'd been with him every minute. But would she recant if pressed?

What if the police came up with a witness to say that Katrine had been on her own for a time? That wouldn't be hard to do. He'd left her at the festival for at least thirty minutes.

Just long enough to...well, long enough to do what needed to be done.

He felt a sudden hyper-sensitivity as he felt his fear ratchet up inside his chest.

What would he do if someone came forward saying they saw Katrine on her own? Or worse, that they'd seen himself with that *connard* Deroy?

Jean-Joseph wracked his brain for his memory of that afternoon as he'd done countless times since the festival to imagine if anyone could possibly have seen him.

29

PIECES OF DREAMS

Mornings at *La Fleurette* are the best.

And that's in spite of the fact that I have my whole laundry list of chores ahead of me. I like mornings the best because my day always starts with an amazing cup of coffee and something flaky and sweet that one of the twins has just pulled out of the oven—warmed up *pain au chocolat*, brioche, or *pain beurre*.

And then my day morphs into at least a few minutes of sitting outside on our terrace and watching how the morning looks in the natural world. This is honestly something I'd never imagined doing back home in Atlanta. Back then I lived in a condo in Buckhead in a very upscale, very urban neighborhood. The only part of the natural world I was aware of back then was the sliver of light between my parking garage and my condo.

I'm not an outdoorsy kind of girl. Or at least, I never used to be.

So how to explain how much I relish these moments wrapped up in a wool rug, my steaming mug of coffee in my hands and my assorted dogs, cats and chickens milling about my feet.

The cats spend the night out every night unless it's freezing so when I get settled ont he terrace with my coffee they're usually lined up on the medieval stone wall licking their paws, washing their faces after a night of terrorizing all the voles and field mice in our garden.

Cocoa, who sleeps on my bed, is less appreciative of these cold mornings but she gamely sniffs at rocks and clumps of dirt until I'm ready to turn my attention back to the house. When that happens, all four of the animals bolt for the house and whatever is sure to await them in their food bowls in the kitchen.

This morning I was thinking of how awesome my mornings are—pre-chores—because I was feeling very appreciative of my life at the moment. As in, *not incarcerated*.

I can't say I was exactly worried about getting nailed for Deroy's murder but I know how easily misunderstandings can happen and also how a thing can look utterly like one thing yet not be true at all.

But spending the bulk of your life in prison, well, I'm sure it sucks even worse if you're innocent.

Marco stepped out onto the terrace with Twig at his heels and his own mug of coffee in his hands. Cocoa dashed over to him assuming he would let her inside.

"*Bonne matin*, Jules," he said, his breath creating fog as he spoke.

"Did you sleep well?" I asked, knowing my brief moment of reflection and peace was now over.

"I did. Thank you. *Les soeurs* want me to bring their wine cases to Thibault's this morning."

I frowned and turned to look at him. "Why can't Thibault come pick them up?"

"I do not know. But it's fine."

"Do you want help hooking Roulette to the cart?"

He hesitated. I knew he'd done it a couple days ago when I was in jail but it's really a two-man job, especially if you don't know what you're doing.

"I don't mind, Marco," I said, standing up and tossing the dregs of my coffee into the rosemary bushes. "It's time to begin the day anyway."

Marco and I really hadn't taken the time to debrief about everything that had gone down yesterday at the police station. Marco is like most men in that he doesn't talk about his feelings very much but I knew that even though he'd broken up with Eloise he was still hurt that she'd not told him she'd been married. Or who knows? Maybe he was feeling guilty about dumping her. Even *I* felt bad after the way Eloise carried on. He'd have to be made of stone for it not to affect him.

"You okay, Marco?" I said as I gave his arm a quick squeeze. His face looked tense and I chided myself for not thinking of what all this was doing to him. In fact, there was a definite argument to be made that I'd kicked this whole mess off when I lied to Eloise last summer and conned her into doing me a favor knowing I had no intention of giving her the thing I'd promised in return.

I wondered for a moment if any part of Marco blamed me for what happened between him and Eloise. I wondered if he ever thought about the fact that I'd made a promise that I didn't keep. Did he see me as double-dealing now? Untrustworthy?

As I watched him ruffle Cocoa's ears before heading back into the house I realized that if he had been upset with how I'd behaved this summer, he'd already forgiven me.

And no offence, Katrine, but that's what real friends do.

Justine opened the door to the house and Cocoa and Twig bounded past her. I could smell the fragrance of the pan of *croissants* just being pulled out of the oven.

Good God, how did I ever live without homemade croissants in the morning?

"Marco, the fire is going out," Justine said taking his coffee mug from him.

"Oops," he said and turned to reverse his steps. "I'll chop more wood."

I stepped into the warm kitchen and saw that the three cats were somehow there ahead of us. Neige, the ringleader and dominant male, Camille, the motherly one but probably the one who called all the shots among them, and Tiny Tim, crippled, shy and by far the sweetest of the three.

Tiny jumped up on the wooden bench by the kitchen table. Léa half turned from the stove without even looking at him, and fed him a tiny piece of sausage.

This family is like nothing I've ever experienced before. It runs as smoothly and involuntarily as breathing in and out. It's always there for you and it never changes. As much as I feel like I stepped into a cocoon of love and acceptance every time I step into the kitchen and into *les soeurs'* orbit, *why today do I feel like there is something unseen in the air poised to ruin it all?*

"You will help Marco hook up the cart?" Léa said over her shoulder to me.

"Of course," I said, folding the wool rug that had been around my shoulders.

"Finish your breakfast," Justine said.

Technically I hadn't started my breakfast but I was not

one to begin the day with a quibble. Léa turned and slid two eggs and a piece of fried toast on my plate.

"*Le confiture* is on the table," she said.

I reached for the jam jar, remembering the day in July when I'd helped the twins cook the raspberries and jar them all up. Summer felt like a long way away.

"So did Sergeant Basile kill him?" Léa asked, her back still to me as she did whatever she was doing at the stove.

"Nobody knows yet."

"I thought it was Monsieur Deschamps who killed him," Justine said, pouring herself a cup of coffee.

"I think he's still in the running," I said around a mouthful of food.

Léa turned to glare at me, a spatula in one hand. "He will have to arrest someone soon."

"Who?" But of course she meant Luc.

"The longer he delays," she said, "the longer his superiors will believe he cannot be impartial about Eloise."

Unspoken but clearly present in the air were the two words she'd left off.

Or you.

Fortunately this less than cheerful moment was interrupted by a surprise knock at our front door. Few things can sidetrack our devoted guard dogs faster than breakfast scraps on the floor so I can't blame poor Cocoa and Twig for falling down on the job. They were both at my heels in full throaty howl as I went to the front door, the feeling of dread rising inside me with every step.

On the doorstep stood Detective Adrien Matteo.

A pair of handcuffs swung from his belt buckle.

30

MILES TO GO

Matteo sat in our kitchen and sipped his coffee. As much as I'm sure the twins wanted to hang around both Justine and Léa decided the detective might be more forthcoming without their presence.

Not that they went far. The pair of them sat quietly in the front salon listening to every word and when Marco came to the back door with an armful of wood, they had him dump the wood in the kitchen and go hook up the horse to the cart on his own.

"*Les soeurs* make the best coffee in all of Chabanel," Matteo said as he slurped his coffee.

"I'll be sure and tell them you said so."

I did not like the fact that Matteo was here. If I weren't still on their suspects' list then shouldn't he be off interviewing the rest of the village or measuring Monsieur Deschamps for a prison jumpsuit?

No, I did not like his presence here one little bit. Had Luc sent him? Did Luc not know he was here? But I hadn't dealt with Matteo with four years and not come out the other side with some semblance of an idea of how to handle him.

And the direct way was almost never the best way with this guy.

"Why didn't Luc come?" I asked.

"Chief DeBray thought it would be best if I came," Matteo said hesitantly.

"Do you know why?" I asked trying to hide the sudden throb of fear that had erupted deep in my gut.

Dear God. Is Luc breaking up with me?

I totally wouldn't blame him. Every time he turns around someone is either dropping dead or I'm being arrested or putting him in some kind of impossible situation. Of *course* he's breaking up with me. What sane man wouldn't?

"I think he believes that...discretion...is best observed at this time," Matteo said.

I tried to determine whether this was Matteo's own interpretation or whether Luc had told him to say it. I mean, it made sense that Luc would want to distance himself from me—at least for the duration of the investigation.

If that's what he's doing.

And if it's just for the duration of the investigation.

"The lab report on the knife came back," Matteo said, clearly ready to change the subject. "There were no prints."

"That's good news, right?"

"For whom?" Matteo asked, making a face. "Not for the police attempting to find the killer."

I guess he had a point. Excuse me for only thinking of myself when it came to incriminating evidence in a murder investigation.

"What about Deschamps? Did you confront him with what Angelique said?"

"Monsieur Deschamps admitted that Deroy had found Angelique in the pasture the day before the festival and attempted to rape her. Deschamps also readily admitted he wanted to kill him but the man ran away. He didn't see him again until the festival when he assaulted him."

"But he didn't kill him?"

"He insists not and his wife continues to support him. She will not recant her statement that her husband was with her the whole time."

"So is that all you have on him? Motive only?"

"It is. All circumstantial. No real evidence."

"Well, who else is there? Surely you're not thinking *Eloise* killed him?"

Matteo shrugged. "Again, as with Deschamps, there is no real evidence against her. It seems that everyone had a good motive for killing the man but no evidence to support it."

"Will this case just go unsolved?"

For a moment it occurred to me that it wouldn't be the worst thing in the world. Nobody knew or liked Deroy. He had no family. What difference did it make if the killer was never found? The killer was probably just some normal upstanding citizen with the misfortune to run into Deroy.

But just like with the murder last spring of a generally despicable man—Fabrice Charlevoix—it tended to bother me to let murderers get away with murder.

I saw Matteo hesitate and wondered if he was about to tell me something he shouldn't. That would be highly unusual for Matteo but with Eloise possibly about to be held on a murder charge, perhaps he was willing to listen to whatever theories *I* might have.

And of course, to hear those, he'd have to share his.

"Chief DeBray is questioning Jean-Joseph Dimer again," he said.

I frowned. "Really? Why?"

"He was seen arguing with Deroy at the festival."

"Boy, you really are desperate, aren't you?"

"Katrine Pelletier swears she was with him every second."

When he said that I came *this* close to blurting out that I knew for a fact that that wasn't true. I just barely managed to stuff the words back in my mouth—as you know an unusual and rare happenstance for me.

But the fact was Katrine and Jean-Joseph *weren't* together when I first saw Katrine at the festival. Katrine's alibi for Jean-Joseph could be shattered by a simple eyewitness testimony that someone had seen Katrine alone and without her boyfriend.

But by hell and damnation it wouldn't be me.

"Did Chief DeBray mention the diary to you that we found in the victim's backpack in the nearby bushes?" Matteo asked, his eyes narrowing at me over his coffee cup.

"Now that you mention it he did say something about a notebook," I said. "Why? What's in the notebook?"

"It appears to reveal an intent to blackmail both Eloise and Marie Dionne although they are not specifically named and no indication of what crimes they were supposed to have committed."

"But we already knew that," I said. "Both Eloise and Marie Dionne have admitted he tried to blackmail them."

"I imagine then that the Chief also told you about the embroidered handkerchief found under the body that was stained with the victim's blood which we now believe was used to wipe the knife of prints."

You know how sometimes you're just sitting there and all

of a sudden the floor seems to drop away and your stomach plummets to the ground?

I cleared my throat. "Embroidered..."

"With the initials JHA," Matteo said, watching my face closely.

Jules Hooker Alaoui

A spasm of nausea fluttered in my stomach and I was suddenly sorry for eating the two fried eggs earlier.

Justine had made me no fewer than a dozen of these handkerchiefs with my initials embroidered on them in her war against my seasonal allergies.

I felt sweat form on my top lip.

"Deroy could have stolen a handkerchief from me at any time," I said. "I only have a dozen of them scattered about the house."

"Of course," Matteo said. "However. It's not good."

I shivered. Even in the heart of the warmest room in the house sometimes a chill can come through this old house that just freezes my blood on contact.

"I'm surprised Eloise didn't jump with both feet on this handkerchief evidence," I said bitterly.

"She probably would have but she didn't know about it. I found it at the murder scene and didn't reveal it to her. When she was taken off the case, I of course could not then share any information with her."

I cocked my head at Matteo. I knew he didn't exactly hate me. He probably didn't have the emotional bandwidth for that. But until this moment I'd never seen any sign of benevolence or magnanimity in him either.

Although there was that eighty-foot fall off a cliff he saved me from once. I guess that counts for magnanimous.

"What about Marie Dionne?" I said feeling flustered with these thoughts of warmth toward Matteo. "Why aren't you talking to her? She was at the festival *and* she was overheard threatening to kill Deroy. What's the hold up?"

"Unfortunately, Mademoiselle Dionne has a withered right hand—the ME says the killer was right-handed—so it seems unlikely she could have done it. I assure you Chief DeBray is working hard to find something to move the focus off you. But I fear the handkerchief when combined with the other evidence...well, it's not good."

You're telling me.

Suddenly I noticed he'd finished his coffee and had appeared to run out of things to say. And then it hit me.

"Are...are you here to arrest me?"

"I was told to go by Madame Pelletier's to bring her with me since we don't have a police woman to accompany you."

"Don't tell me. She wouldn't come."

"I regret to say she wouldn't. I am therefore not comfortable bringing you in without a female escort."

I felt a flush of relieved bewilderment. Matteo was cutting me a break and he didn't have to. Did I mention I nearly married this guy? *Plus* he saved my life?

I feel downright ashamed for not really liking him.

It was right about then that both twins couldn't take it any longer and they charged into the kitchen saying that they had been with me the whole time at the festival. I appreciated what they were trying to do but as Matteo pointed out there were already too many people who'd seen me wandering about on my own that afternoon.

Léa gave me a fierce look as if I should have known better than to not be some place where she could conveniently alibi me.

Honestly it was hard to concentrate on what anyone was saying at the moment—and this particular moment was all about whether or not I would be arrested and dragged down to the jail in the village.

But I couldn't help flashing back to an image of Katrine turning down Matteo's request that she accompany him to *La Fleurette*.

If it's not for our friends, what's it all for? If Katrine thinks I did this—or worse, if she doesn't—and she's still not willing to help me, what is the point of loving someone?

I'm sure I was giving this a way less positive read than I should have. But this felt worse than being snubbed in the village square or refusing to talk to me at a party. This went straight to the heart of my belief in sisterhood and friendship, something that I've learned in my short time in France goes beyond blood.

It goes straight to the heart of that belief.

And bludgeons it until it's a battered, bloody pulp.

I pulled myself out of these black thoughts in time to hear both Justine and Léa begging Matteo not to take me away. I hated to hear them so upset and I guess Matteo did too because he held up both hands to insist on silence.

"Promise me she will not leave," he said to Léa. Although God knows I have no idea why he would look to *Léa* of all people for this kind of assurance. The woman is the biggest dissembler I know. If she thinks a thing must be done she would certainly never let a little thing like *her word* stand in the way.

Nonetheless, Léa nodded solemnly at him.

"She will not leave, Detective Matteo," she said. "I swear this on my brother's grave."

She doesn't have a brother.

Matteo frowned for a moment, probably because he never remembered there being any brother either, but he nodded anyway.

He turned to me.

"We are all doing everything we can to find the real killer," he said, making me believe in spite of the evidence that he doesn't think the killer was me.

A ringing testimonial if I'd ever heard one.

"Don't make me lose my trust in *les soeurs*," he said to me.

"Of course not," I said, trying to keep a straight face and receiving a very unpleasant kick under the table from Léa for my efforts.

After I'd walked him to the door and watched him get on his bike to make the trip back to Chabanel, I stood there and stared out and I'm ashamed to say I didn't feel relieved or grateful at my reprieve. Not at all.

I felt destroyed.

I had lost Katrine. And now I knew she was never coming back.

31

LIKE A SHOT TO THE HEART

The rest of the day unfolded the way most of them do at *La Fleurette*—except with a definite patina of despondency for me. The twins knew something was bothering me but I was smart enough not to say anything since Léa especially would be relentless in her pronouncement that I was an ingrate and not deserving of all the gifts that fell in my lap.

I know if you'd survived torture and concentration camps in your life the fact that a friend turned her back on you might not qualify as a major life crisis but for me and my basically charmed life, it was a killer.

And I was struggling.

After I fed the animals and weeded the garden for a few hours Marco had returned from delivering the wine to Thibault. I never did hear why Thibault couldn't swing by and pick up the wine but since Marco didn't seem to mind, I didn't ask. Thibault is a dear friend of mine and I think he'd give an arm for me, but he is inordinately secretive and asking him why he did something was as useless as trying to hang the moon. In heels.

Trust me, I've attempted both.

Marco may not be as callous to my moods as *les soeurs* but even he knew something was wrong and eventually—when we were both in the middle of cleaning out Roulette's stall—he asked me about it.

"I thought you would be happy not to be arrested by Detective Matteo," he said as he pitchforked dirty hay into the back of a large wheelbarrow.

"I am happy."

"You don't look it."

Honestly, neither did Marco. I know this whole mess with Eloise was probably harder on him than I'd given him credit for. Marco is a simple creature. Not unlike my dog, he likes to please and he basks in the resultant praise. Moreover, he doesn't like to make people unhappy or God forbid, cry.

I wasn't used to a sad Marco. It kind of broke my heart.

"Why is the Chief not visiting us?" he asked suddenly.

So he'd noticed that too.

When I wasn't wrestling with my dilemma over Katrine ending our friendship, I was dwelling on the fact that Luc hadn't come to debrief with me—or even send me a message. It made sense what Matteo had said—that Luc was trying to downplay his connection with me for the duration of the case. Obviously Luc has his superiors breathing down his neck and he already had at least one formal complaint of bias against him.

I get it. I do.

Sort of.

Marco jammed the pitchfork into the ground and turned to sit on one of the hay bales.

"What can make us feel better?" he said sadly.

In that moment, he looked like a little boy who'd lost his

favorite toy. I sat next to him and put my arms around him. And then suddenly I snapped my fingers.

"That's it!" I said.

He looked at me in surprise. "What?"

"We need to find Deroy's killer. That's what will fix everything."

Well, not my problems with Katrine but two out of three...

"But how? You heard Detective Matteo. They have suspects with motive but no evidence."

"That has literally never stopped me before," I said, as I stood up and felt a rush as my brain began to kick in gear. "Okay. What do we know about the murder?"

Marco seemed to perk up too. "He was killed with your utility knife."

"Okay. Good. And who had access to my knife?"

Marco frowned.

"Everyone did," I said. "Don't you see? Deroy stole the knife so he was literally carrying the murder weapon around with him. All the killer had to do was take it from him and use it on him."

Marco's frown increased. "So is that good?"

"I don't know," I admitted. "What else?"

"Everyone hated him?"

"Yes! Yes, that's good, Marco. He was a stranger in town and yet he succeeded in alienating a large number of people."

"That's why they all have motive," Marco said. His eyes were hopeful but clearly not yet seeing where any of this was going.

"They do, yes," I said and then began ticking the names off my hands. "His stepsister Marie Dionne, motive and opportunity but not means. Monsieur Deschamps, likewise motive, and means but not opportunity—if his wife is to be believed. Eloise, motive, opportunity and possibly means—but no evidence to support it."

"Katrine Pelletier's boyfriend," Marco said excitedly.

"That's right," I said. "He was seen arguing with Deroy *and* he had opportunity and means, but we don't know about motive."

We paused for a moment.

"And of course myself," I said.

"Jules, don't," Marco said, glowering. "We know it wasn't you so why add yourself to the list?"

I shrugged. "Only because it helps me see how we all stack up against one another."

I caught a glimpse of movement and saw Justine open the back door of the house and start down the path toward us. She had a basket over one arm and I wondered if she was going to cut flowers or pick tomatoes. Amazingly, there were still a few left on the vine.

"You should add Theo to the list," Marco said.

I watched Justine pick her way down the path. She looked a little more frail, I thought with surprise. Everyone believed she'd totally recovered from the accident last summer and on the face of it you couldn't really see much difference. But she was moving slower. And she looked thinner too.

"Yes, good," I said absently. "Theo fought with Deroy too, didn't he?"

"And he was at the festival," Marco said. "So he had opportunity."

"No," I said. "Opportunity means he had the space of time to commit the crime and it turns out that Theo didn't. I'm not really sure he had motive either. Just because he argued with Deroy the day before isn't really a motive for murder."

"Except Theo isn't acting like himself these days," Marco said, standing up and picking up the pitchfork again.

I looked at him. "So you've noticed?"

"After you said something I started watching him and you're right, he's different. Angrier, sadder."

Justine waved to us and I trotted up the path to greet her.

"Are you picking the last of the tomatoes?" I asked. "Do you want me to do it?"

"No, *chérie*," she said, her smile reaching her eyes as she regarded me. "I want to be outdoors for a bit."

I couldn't help but think I wanted her to be sitting on the terrace with the late afternoon sun on her face and a wool rug across her lap, not exerting herself.

"I am glad to see your mood is better," she said. "What are you and Marco talking about so earnestly?"

"We're trying to figure out who could have killed René Deroy."

"Léa and I both put our money on Theo Bardot," she said.

"I can't believe you said that! We were just talking about Theo but it can't be him."

"Oh?"

"No, he wasn't out of Detective Matteo's sight during the whole festival. And when he was, he was passed out drunk."

Justine arched an eyebrow which is *les soeurs*-speak for *that convinces me of nothing.*

Trust me I could write a dictionary on their nonverbal cues.

"Do you know something, Justine?" I asked.

"Detective Matteo certainly did not have eyes on Monsieur Bardot the whole time," she said.

"He says he did."

"That is because Detective Matteo is embarrassed about

the twenty minutes he spent in the *pissoir* recovering from the after-effects of a bad oyster."

I stared at her.

Matteo *didn't* have eyes on Theo the whole time?

"How do you know this?" I said, my heart pounding.

"Léa and I witnessed the detective bolting for the WC."

Twenty minutes was plenty of time to do the deed.

"But Matteo said that Theo was drunk the whole time," I said.

"A state of true drunkenness is most often only accurately discernible to the one who is intoxicated, wouldn't you say?"

"You mean you think Theo could have been faking it."

"It is just a theory, *chérie*," she said with a smile as she turned toward the garden and the last tomatoes of the season.

I walked back to where Marco was finishing with a final forkful of dirty hay.

"Theo doesn't have an alibi," I said to him. "Justine just told me that Matteo was sick for twenty minutes and nobody was watching Theo during that time."

"What does this mean?" Marco grabbed the handles of the wheelbarrow. I hurried to open the shed door for him as he maneuvered the loaded wheelbarrow through it.

My mind was buzzing as I watched Marco stop the wheelbarrow at the back of the shed and begin to scrape the manure and soiled hay into a huge pile we kept back there.

Theo had a run-in with Deroy.

Theo was unstable these days.

Theo had motive, opportunity and means.

I shook my head. There still needed to be something concrete.

"Oh, *mon Dieu*," Marco said.

I snapped my head up. "What? What is it?"

He turned and sat down hard on the side of the wheelbarrow.

"I just remembered something," he said. He looked like he was going to be sick. "You said they found your handkerchief under the body?"

I felt my whole body begin to tingle and somehow I just knew that what he had to tell me was going to change everything.

"Yes," I said slowly.

He shook his head and I saw his eyes glisten as if he were getting emotional.

"Last week at the café Theo fell asleep at one of the outdoor tables." Marco took a long breath. "He...he was drooling. I thought he would be embarrassed if he...if people could see him like that."

"You wiped away the drool," I said.

He looked at me and nodded miserably. "With one of your handkerchiefs. I don't even know why I had it on me."

"Because I leave them all over the house."

He stared at his hands in the picture of dejection.

"I put the handkerchief in his shirt pocket thinking he might need it again."

Theo had motive, means, opportunity and the handkerchief he left at the scene of the crime after he used it to wipe his fingers off the murder weapon.

I stared at Marco for a moment, my mind swimming with what I now knew.

Theo was the killer.

32

HELL IN A HAND BASKET

When it really hit me that Theo was the killer I just gaped at Marco in shock. Bless his heart, it took Marco a little longer to catch up. But when he did, the realization slammed into him like a slap in the face.

"Can it really be him?" he said with a gasp.

I didn't bother answering but turned and ran to the paddock where Roulette was grazing. I had to get into town. I had to tell Luc. I grabbed Roulette's saddle pad and saddle and hurried into his enclosure.

"Jules, wait!" Marco said. "Where are you going?"

Suddenly I knew it wasn't Luc I had to see but Theo himself. I needed him to confess what he'd done.

Marco jogged over to me as I tossed the saddle pad on Roulette.

"Hand me his bridle, will you?" I said breathlessly as I eased the saddle over Roulette's withers and onto his back. I quickly fastened the cinch. I pulled Roulette's halter off and dropped it on the ground by my feet.

Marco hesitated and then went back to the shed.

"You are going to tell the Chief?" he said, handing me the bridle.

I slipped the bridle over Roulette's nose. For being a pill in every other regard and with as much as he doesn't particularly enjoy being ridden Roulette tended to be easy to tack up.

I was especially thankful for that today.

"No," I said, grabbing the reins and positioning my foot in the stirrup. "I'm going to tell *Theo* what I know." I swung into the saddle.

Marco grabbed the bridle with both hands but when Roulette tossed his head in annoyance, Marco let go. He wasn't comfortable around horses.

"Jules, you can't!" he said, the tendons standing out on his neck. "If Theo is the killer you will be in danger."

I pulled Roulette's head toward the paddock gate. Marco stood in front of me, blocking my path.

"No, Jules! I can't let you go!"

I'm not sure what I would have said to Marco at that point. I didn't feel like I had all the time in the world but I suppose I would have done my best to convince him to let me go.

As it happened I didn't have to.

I heard the scream at the same time Roulette shied violently beneath me, nearly unseating me.

"Whoa, boy," I said, trying to keep my voice calm.

I twisted in the saddle to see where the scream had come from. I saw the figure sitting on the roof waving to us. Léa had been saying for a week that she was going to go up there and pull the leaves out of the drains. I'm surprised she did it herself when she had Marco to do it but I have long since stopped trying to figure out Léa's motivations for anything she does.

"The ladder fell!" she called to us.

I glanced at Marco and saw the tortured indecision in his face.

"Help her off the roof," I said firmly to him. "I'll be fine."

"Jules, I wish you—"

"Marco!" Léa shouted. "Get over here *now*!"

Before Marco had a chance to decide what to do I made it easy on him. I put my heels to Roulette and bolted past him and out of the paddock.

"I'll be fine!" I called over my shoulder. "Go rescue the crazy lady on the roof!"

It had been too long since I'd let Roulette really go and he was more than ready now. We hit the dirt road outside our *mas* at a canter and he quickly transitioned to a gallop for the rest of the way to town.

For once, I let him do it. It would not only get us there faster but would take some of the pent-up energy out of him.

As we pelted down the straightest part of the village road, pastures on either side of me flying by, I felt the cold October wind slamming through me.

As soon as I hit the village I forced Roulette into the most miserable trot I've ever experienced but I was too excited to walk and it was too dangerous to canter within the village. As I rode, I spent a few moments rehearsing what I would say to Theo.

I needed him to realize that there was no point in denying it. Once I got him to that point, I'd hand him over to Luc and Matteo so they could do all the formal cop stuff. A part of me was really sorry this was all happening. Theo had been, if not a friend to me, at least friendly and he'd given

Marco a job when he needed it. I hated that it was going down like this. It would have been much better if a total stranger had killed Deroy.

I was twenty yards from the front of the café terrace when I could see that it was closed. I literally cannot remember a time when the café was closed.

I shouldn't have been surprised. After all, Marco was at *La Fleurette* and Theo had become less and less capable of handling the running of the café on his own. I have to say it was at this point that I began to wonder who would get the café—and the bar—after Theo went down for Murder One. Things were looser these days after the EMP. Ownership lines were sketchier. It was entirely possible that Marco might get the café, at least to manage.

I swung down from Roulette and tied him to a wooden parking bar in front of the café. I pounded on the door and peered in the big picture window that faced the square. It was dimly lit inside but I thought I could tell there was nobody there.

Tamping down a feeling of frustration, I turned and faced the square and my eyes landed on the city hall. While it was true Theo had been less than inclined in his duties as mayor, it probably wouldn't hurt to at least check his office. Besides, I'd have to run by the police station anyway to get Matteo or Luc to open up Theo's café just in case he was out of view somewhere on the premises.

I hurried over to the city hall and ran up the steps. The mayor's secretary, Madame LaTour, looked up from her desk as I walked in.

I don't have a real good relationship with Madame LaTour. She practically worked as the last mayor's henchman in trying to kill me—and yes I know that's a slight exaggeration—plus she's vehemently anti-American.

Not to mention that when Katrine was running for mayor I made it clear to any and all who'd listen that Katrine's first chore as mayor should be to fire Madame LaTour. It's one thing to know where the bodies are buried, it's quite another to have helped bury them.

"*Bonjour*, Madame LaTour," I said. "I am looking for Theo."

The old woman pushed her crossword puzzle aside and snorted in response but otherwise didn't answer.

"I have urgent information to share with the mayor," I said, not sure if LaTour was loyal to Theo—or even really acquainted with him. "It's vital that I see him immediately."

"Then that is too bad for you," she said.

I started to walk past her desk although I knew this was a waste of time. Theo hadn't been interested in being mayor and I couldn't imagine he'd spent any time in city hall, let alone be here now.

"Mayor Bardot is not here!" she screeched.

I turned to look at her.

She knew something. About Theo.

"Where is he?" I asked.

"I do not know."

She did too know. Remember how I said I learned to size up certain people after living in a village for four years? Well, just like Madame Gabin likes to hear gossip, this old broad likes to spread it. For my purposes, that means she keeps her ear to the floor *and* the wall.

"Katrine Pelletier is filing a no-confidence measure against the mayor," I said. That was a lie but now that I thought about it, it wasn't a bad idea.

Nobody credible could possibly come forward to support Theo as being anything but an absentee mayor.

Madame LaTour spat at my feet, totally surprising me.

Up until then I'd assumed she cared about maintaining at least a veneer of propriety.

"Mayor Bardot will take care of Madame Pelletier *and* her no-confidence measure," she said.

There was something about the way Madame LaTour said the words and the way she glanced out the window toward the café as she said them that made me think this was not an idle threat.

It sounded like she'd actually heard a threat against Katrine.

By Theo.

"If Theo Bardot harms Katrine," I said, "he'll get a whole lot worse than just a no-confidence measure. You can count on that."

Did Madame LaTour know that Theo had killed Deroy? Did she suspect?

"What do you know, Madame LaTour? What did Theo tell you?"

She smiled her evil smile and sat back in her chair.

"He said he was going to take care of Katrine Pelletier," she said. "Once and for all."

33

ALL YOU NEED IS LOVE

Theo stepped behind the tree where he could see them bette. They'd been so focused on themselves they hadn't looked around once. They had no idea someone might be watching them.

Following them.

He could see Katrine as she clung to the man's arm but he couldn't hear her voice. Only the man spoke, loudly and nonstop.

Theo cringed to think that Katrine really preferred this man.

Had could I have been so wrong about her?

The pair hesitated at the edge of the forest which made Theo frown. He'd been ecstatic to have spotted them as they made their way out of the village on foot, the bulky picnic hamper between them leaving no doubt as to what they were up to.

And would there be a blanket to spread on the forest floor? Theo wondered in mounting disgust and fury.

As the two paused before entering the forest, Theo pulled out a flask and drank down its contents. Irritated

Wined and Died

with how little there was left in the flask, he tossed it in the bushes where he had hidden his bicycle.

He narrowed his eyes at the couple. They seemed to be arguing about something. The picnic basket was on the ground now between them.

No, it was still only the man talking. Katrine was listening, her head bowed.

The man's voice raised up and Theo heard him curse.

He was unhappy with Katrine about something. He was shouting at her.

Would they cancel their picnic? Would they turn back?

Theo sent up a desperate prayer that they wouldn't.

They had to go on.

He was ready to do it today.

For the love of God, he couldn't wait any longer or he would lose his mind.

Suddenly, he watched the man snatch up the picnic basket and stomp into the forest. For a moment it looked as if Katrine might not follow him. But then she did.

Slowly and with resignation, she disappeared behind him into the dark shadow of the forest.

Theo smiled with satisfaction.

He counted to fifty.

And then followed them.

34

BUSTING A MOVE

Eloise sat on the bench under the plane trees that bordered the village square. She'd been sitting there nearly an hour when she saw Jules ride up and peer into the closed café windows.

Just look at her walking around like she owns the town.

She wasn't surprised that Jules didn't see her as she strode across the square to the city hall. Eloise was as immovable as the statue erected to memorialize the war dead that she sat beside. She was however surprised to see Jules go to the city hall instead of the police station. But not by much.

She is always sticking her nose into everyone's business. She probably thinks she should be the mayor of Chabanel now.

A clutch of panic pierced her.

Would Luc allow that? Would Jules become the town's next mayor?

Eloise knew for a fact that Jules could and there was nothing Eloise could do about it.

Suddenly Jules emerged from the city hall and turned for the police station next door.

Naturally.

A stab of outrage jettisoned Eloise to her feet and she dropped her bottle of *pastis* to the cobblestones with a shattering crash.

Someone has to stop her, she thought as she forced her legs to move across the uneven pavers to the police station. *Someone has to do what's right for Chabanel.*

And I am the only one who can.

She walked up the flat broad stairs of the police station and flung open the door, already steeling herself against the disapproving glare she knew Madame Gabin would give her.

Jules was leaning on the front of the receptionist's desk, her stance the picture of impatience.

And Madame Gabin was *listening* to her.

"If you won't let me talk to Matteo," Jules said to Madame Gabin, "then tell him he needs to go check the café for Theo."

"The chief of police is usually the one who tells our detectives what they need to do," Madame Gabin said but her eyes flicked past Jules to Eloise as she approached.

Jules turned around and when she saw Eloise her eyes reflected surprise but no real interest.

That was the final straw.

The disrespect that this interloper could look at her and not care or worry what I thought was just too much.

In a flash, the only thing Eloise could see was the vivid image of her fingernails raking bloody creases down the American's smug, disgusting face.

Everything else dissolved into a swirl of red-hot hatred... the reception room, the sound of voices, even the ticking of the station clock.

It was all gone in the moment Eloise launched herself at Jules...

...her nails extended toward the American like a falcon's talons.

35

TICK TOCK

What a total whack-job!

As soon as I saw Eloise come at me, I side-stepped and she ended up sprawled across Madame Gabin's desk.

At least it was a sure-fire way to get Matteo to come out and talk to me.

He stood here now, one hand on Eloise—because if you can believe this, she was still trying to take a swing at me—and glaring at both of us.

"Don't look at me like that," I said to him. "She came at *me*!"

"She wants to be mayor of Chabanel!" Eloise shrieked, spittle flying from her lips.

"Okay, so she's totally lost the plot," I said with disgust before turning to Matteo. "Listen, Adrien, I need you to check out the café to make sure Theo isn't in there drowning in his own vomit."

I wasn't at all ready to reveal to Matteo or anyone else my suspicions about Theo—not until I had an ironclad confession in my back pocket.

"Monsieur Bardot is not in his café," Matteo said. "I witnessed him riding his bike not thirty minutes ago."

Riding his bike?

"What direction?" I asked.

"That is none of your concern," Matteo said flatly, his Mister-Nice-Guy persona now officially Mister-Way-Gone now.

He had to readjust his grip on Eloise because she kept squirming and while I didn't envy him the rest of his afternoon dealing with her, it was annoying that cleaning up the mess that was Eloise was going to take precedence over finding Deroy's killer.

"Where's Luc?" I asked.

"Working," Matteo said, his mouth in a firm line. That was obviously all I was getting from him.

"Fine. Just keep that nut job away from me," I said nodding at Eloise before turning and exiting the building.

I stood outside on the front steps for a few moments, trying to think what to do next.

If Theo left the area on a bike that must mean wherever he was going was further than walking distance. Did this mean he wasn't stinking drunk? Although honestly I've seen Frenchmen ride bikes when you'd swear they were absolutely hammered.

Probably a skill they all learn at a young age.

I went to untie Roulette and felt a throb of unease in my gut.

Should I have told Matteo about the threat LaTour said Theo made against Katrine?

No, without any real evidence it was just she-said-he-said.

I need to find Theo.

I swung up into the saddle and the sudden movement seemed to energize me.

Theo was on a bike, probably not all that drunk, and he had gone to "take care" of Katrine.

I turned Roulette's head in the direction of the Chabanel village church, behind which was a neighborhood where Katrine lived with her mother.

36

ALL FALL DOWN

Katrine listened to Jean-Joseph's complaints as if they were so many pebbles raining down on her. It took all of her endurance to continue to walk deeper and deeper into the forest. Had she ever told him that she'd once been attacked in this forest? Or that she'd gotten lost in it as a child? Or that she used to have nightmares about being imprisoned by its fir trees?

Of course not. She'd not even told Gaultier. Or her own mother.

Or Jules.

It had just been so easy over the years to simply not go anywhere near the forest than to face what it meant to her—the center of all that was terrifying.

So why had she agreed to come here today?

Why was she walking along the forest trail, her eyes darting everywhere at once in anticipation of snakes? Why was she accompanying Jean-Joseph when every fiber of her being told her to turn and run back to the pasture?

Why? Because her mother had told her that Jean-Joseph intended to propose to her today.

Her stomach lurched uncomfortably at the thought.

Jean-Joseph would get a job. He'd only been in the village a short time. He would find work. And then he would help Katrine support her children. She would be able to move out of her mother's apartment.

And then she would be married again. She would be respectable again. The distance between her and her first husband would grow until nobody would remember what happened to him. Or that she'd ever been connected to him.

"Are you listening to me?" Jean-Joseph said, the frustration evident in his voice.

Katrine tore her eyes away from the ground which any minute might start writhing with woodland vipers and glanced worriedly at Jean-Joseph.

"What?" she said.

"You're not listening to me!" he said as he dropped the picnic basket dramatically on the ground. "I said the only reason the stupid police chief is even *looking* at me is because *you* weren't believable when you told him I was with you every minute at the festival!"

Katrine blinked and looked about in confusion.

"Did you hear what I said?"

"Yes, Jean-Joseph, but I don't know what to say to you."

"You admit you didn't try very hard to cover for me!" He snatched a heavy stick from a nearby bush and stabbed the ground with it to punctuate his words.

"I...I did my best."

"Your *best* might get me put in jail like your first husband! Is that what you want? Is that your thing? Your *best* might be making sure any man stupid enough to be caught with you ends up serving prison time!" Jean-Joseph struck a nearby sapling with the stick and made a shower of dead leaves dump down onto the path.

A thin layer of perspiration popped out on Katrine's upper lip. She thought she heard a noise coming from the bushes. Were there bears in this part of France? Wolves?

She looked around. "Maybe we should go back," she said timidly.

"Are you serious?" Jean-Joseph shouted. "We're on a picnic, you stupid woman!"

Why is he so angry? Katrine wondered, feeling her heart thump loudly in her throat. There was that noise again. Was it closer this time?

She took a step backward and suddenly felt an overwhelming urge to just turn and run.

Whatever was out there in the bushes...whatever it was...it was waiting for her...

She stumbled another step backward and reached for a sapling to keep from falling.

"Look out what you're...Hey, what are *you* doing here?" Jean-Joseph said.

Katrine felt an army of spiders crawling up her back at the change in Jean-Joseph's voice. She forced herself to turn and look.

Theo Bardot, looking unsteady on his feet, stood directly in front of Jean-Joseph. His hands were clenching and unclenching at his side, his eyes were unfocused.

Dear God, he's in a drunken rage, Katrine thought, fighting to get her breath. She stumbled again and this time lost her footing and fell to her knees.

"Get out of here!" Jean-Joseph screamed at Theo. "You...you pervert!"

Katrine watched in horror as Theo, his face contorted in murderous intent, reached for Jean-Joseph.

And then Katrine saw Jean-Joseph bring the stick whistling through the air to slam into Theo's face.

37
A DAY LATE

Luc walked to where the outskirts of the *Mégisseries* met with the edge of the village of Chabanel proper. Normally he'd have driven but in this section of the village that was just asking for trouble. It wasn't as if the denizens of the *Mégisseries* hated the law exactly although that was probably true.

His interview with Marie Dionne had gone about as he'd expected.

In regards to Deroy's murder she was alternately angry and unrepentant. One look at her withered right hand—which she said Deroy caused when as a vicious fifteen-year-old he tried to burn their house down—underscored to Luc that she had motive for killing him in abundance.

Just zero means or ability.

Unless she hired the murder out as a hit. But if her living situation was any indication, she didn't have the money for that. There was just no way Marie Dionne had murdered René Deroy.

Just shows how desperate I am, he thought wearily, a hollowness forming in his chest.

As he walked back toward Chabanel, he noticed a few more people peeking out at him from doorways. There had been very little trouble in the *Mégisseries* in the past few years which didn't surprise him. Everyone was just scrabbling to make ends meet these days.

As he left the poor neighborhood behind he was already angry at himself for wasting precious time on a lead that had never really been a lead at all.

Matteo had told him that Marie couldn't have done it, but Luc had needed to confirm that for himself.

He felt a pulse of anxiety. If he didn't pinpoint a suspect for Deroy's murder soon HQ would send someone else down to "assist." And this time Luc wouldn't have the choice of whether or not to accept the help. All he had to show at the moment was a case with very little evidence but what there was of it pointing directly at Jules.

As Luc entered the first street leading into Chabanel, he saw an elderly man walking away from him with a baguette under his arm. On impulse, Luc decided to stop at the *boulangerie* on the way back to the police station for a bag of *chouquettes*.

It might not solve anything but it certainly couldn't hurt either.

The Chabanel bakery was busy at this time of the day as he could see by the line of half a dozen women standing at the bakery counter.

Luc hesitated outside the door, hating the fact that if he entered the shop his order would be taken in front of all these women who'd been waiting.

"After you, Chief," a cheery voice rang out behind him.

Luc turned to see the elderly retired village schoolteacher Madame Bree standing behind him with an empty basket over her arm and her eyes glittering with good humor.

"*Bonjour*, Madame Bree," he said. "I'm not sure I'm going in after all."

"I am sure Madame Fournier would not make you wait. Or is that the problem?"

Bemused at how quickly she had detected the reason for his hesitation, Luc made a sweeping gesture to allow her to go before him.

"I'll come another time when it is not so busy," he said with a smile.

"Oh! I hope Detective Matteo is fully recovered from the incident at the festival last week?" she said.

"The incident?" Luc frowned. *Was she talking about the murder?*

"I heard it was food poisoning." She called to the line ahead. "Nicole! Didn't you hear that Detective Matteo was terribly indisposed at the festival?"

Nicole turned around, her grey curls bobbing as she nodded her head.

"Yes. Explosive diarrhea," Nicole said sagely. "My Michel witnessed it himself. Is the detective better now?"

"Well, it's a good thing he sorted himself out *before* they found the dead body!" Madame Bree chortled and was soon joined by two other women in line who evidently thought the whole matter equally hilarious.

Luc stared at them, his mouth open in shock.

38

HALF BAKED

Katrine's mother's late nineteenth century apartment building, where Katrine and her two small daughters now lived, was one of the newer structures in Chabanel. It was set off from the rest of Chabanel and—if you can imagine—had been mainly used before the EMP as a space for parties and wedding receptions. There had been a few luxury apartments inside but no full-time residents.

Until Katrine's mother Suzanne moved in.

I tied Roulette up at an iron bar which jutted out from a small defunct fountain in front of the apartment building and strode to the front door. In the old days, you'd use a magnetic key to open the main front door but since nothing worked anymore after the EMP, now you gained entrance via a wedge of wood jammed into the door that held it open. What people were willing to sacrifice in the way of security these days they gained in convenient access.

I opened the door and stepped inside.

Because of Katrine's contentious relationship with her mother I'd only been here a few times. The apartment is—

make no mistake—*Suzanne's* apartment and Katrine and her girls only visitors. I never felt comfortable coming here and I could only imagine what it was like for poor Katrine to *live* here.

I knocked on the first door I came to which was opened immediately by Katrine's ten-year old daughter Babette.

"Hey, Babette," I said cheerfully, glancing past her to see if Katrine was visible. "Your mom home?"

"*Grandmère!*" Babette yelled, her eyes wide as she focused on my face.

This was somewhat unusual behavior since while both girls are intensely shy, I've always gotten along well with them.

Not so today.

Katrine's mother Suzanne, appeared from behind Babette, her expression severe and intractable.

"What do you want?" she said.

Suzanne had probably been pretty at one time but the lines in her face had settled into battle-hardened rows that revealed decades of frowning and grimaces. Even the prettiest face doesn't stand a chance against that.

"Katrine here?"

"My daughter isn't interested in seeing you." Suzanne started to close the door but I stuck my foot out and stopped it.

"I have reason to believe that Katrine is in danger," I said hurriedly. "I need to know where she is, please."

"Danger?" Suzanne snorted. "She is in no danger. Unless it's from her continued association with you."

Wow. This woman seriously hates me. No wonder Katrine hasn't found it in her heart to forgive me yet.

"What is your problem?" I said in frustration. "What did I ever do to you?"

"Do? You turned my daughter into a prison-widow. You made a fool of her in front of the whole village. That's all! You forced her to live on the charity of the village—and me!"

"How the hell did I do that?" I have to say that every one of these so-called crimes was a complete surprise to me. Did Katrine think this way too?

"Because of what you did to Gaultier," Suzanne said with a sneer, "you made all of our lives worse."

"You put our Papa in prison!" Little Odette said from behind Suzanne. "We hate you!"

I have no idea how the truth about what happened to their father somehow got distorted to the point where *I* was the bad guy but I did know I wasn't going to get it sorted it out standing on Suzanne's doorstep.

I forced down the feeling of hurt at the child's words and turned back to Suzanne.

"Someone is trying to harm Katrine," I said between clenched teeth. "Tell me where she is."

"She doesn't need you to save her!" Suzanne said. "She has Jean-Joseph now and he will protect her."

"It will be easier to do that," I said evenly, "if he is warned of the danger."

"No," Suzanne said firmly. "We are not falling for your lies. Jean-Joseph is asking her to marry him today in a lovely picnic in the forest. If you interfere, if you dare to interfere when she is finally getting her life back on track, I will tell the police that I saw you with the murdered man at the festival! I will say I saw you murder him!"

I swear I don't remember the steps it took me to get out of that building and back to where I'd tied up Roulette. Shaken, I did allow myself a moment, with my hands on the saddle and my head pressed against his side, to recover from the terrible things that Katrine's mother had said to me.

And then I took a deep breath.

She said they'd gone to the forest. There weren't too many places suitable for a picnic there. But I think I knew where most of those places were.

I swung back up into the saddle and put my heels to my horse's flank.

39

THE FIERCEST WINDMILLS

Luc slammed his fist against the antique wardrobe in Matteo's office.

"So because you were embarrassed by a case of the runs," he shouted, "you decided not to mention that Theo Bardot was actually *not* being watched continuously?"

"Chief! I wasn't gone for that long," Matteo said, running his tongue over his lips. "And Theo was drunk! I told you!"

"What you *didn't* tell me was that he no longer has an alibi, Detective."

As angry as Luc was to learn that the one man they'd struck off their list should never have been eliminated, he had to admit he was grateful to once more have a possible suspect that wasn't Jules.

They hadn't even questioned Theo!

"You're grasping at straws, Chief! He's the town drunk! He couldn't have done it."

"Of course he could have done it! He was seen having an altercation with the victim the day before the murder and his whereabouts cannot now be verified for the time of the murder!"

Matteo hung his head and for a moment Luc nearly felt sorry for him.

Right up until he thought of how all this was hanging around Jules' neck when all along Theo made much more sense as the killer.

"Get Theo Bardot in here *now*," Luc said.

Matteo stood up. "I'm not sure where he is," he said uncertainly. "I...he was seen leaving on his bike."

Madame Gabin appeared in the doorway.

"Chief," she said, "you should know that Jules Hooker was here thirty minutes ago and she was also looking for Theo Bardot."

Jules must have heard—probably through *les soeurs'* grapevine—that Matteo's alibi for Theo was nonexistent.

If Jules was looking for Theo and Theo was their murderer...

"Chief," Madame Gabin said. "I think you should know that according to Theo Bardot's secretary Madame LaTour, Monsieur Bardot has developed an unhealthy obsession with Katrine Pelletier."

"What?" Luc said in frustration. "Why are you telling me this? Did Katrine make a complaint? Or is this just village gossip?"

Madame Gabin drew herself up in indignation. "There is no formal complaint that I know of."

"Then excuse me, Madame Gabin, but I have a murderer to catch."

"Chief," Matteo said. "If what Madame Gabin says is true and Theo has a dangerous obsession with Katrine Pelletier—"

"Who said he has a dangerous obsession?" Luc said, grabbing his car keys from the peg board in the hall. "Make an effort not to get sidetracked by village gossip, Matteo. I'm disappointed in you."

Luc's mind was buzzing with the image of Jules racing after Theo on his bike to God knows where.

Why hadn't she come to me first when she found out Theo's alibi was no good?

He turned back to Matteo. "Did you tell Jules which way Theo went?"

"No, Chief," Matteo said.

Luc was grateful for that at least. But knowing Jules, it wouldn't slow her down for long.

"And you have no idea where he was going?" Luc asked Matteo.

"He was a man on a bike," Matteo said in bewilderment. "Why would I think twice of it?"

"Check out the café to make sure Theo didn't come back and pass out there," Luc said. "I'll see if any of his drinking buddies have seen him."

"I am just an old woman who gossips," Madame Gabin said, "but if *I* were looking for a man who was obsessed with a woman, I would start with the *woman*."

Luc glanced around the office. "Has Eloise been back in?"

Luc noticed that Matteo shot a guilty look at Madame Gabin before answering.

"She was in earlier," Matteo said, "but I took her home. She was not feeling well."

He means she was drunk, Luc thought in disgust. But at least he wouldn't have to deal with her nonsense at the moment. He'd finally wheedled out of her the information Deroy had felt he could blackmail her with which was the fact that Eloise had once sold drugs as a teen. It wasn't the worst thing she could have done and she was never arrested for it so there was no record.

But it still wasn't good.

In any case, he didn't have time to think about Eloise or her problems right now. He turned toward the door.

"Where are you going, Chief?" Matteo asked. "We still have no idea where Theo went."

"You heard Madame Gabin," Luc said grimly. "I'm looking for the woman Theo is looking for."

40

DO NOT GO GENTLE

The forest that hemmed Chabanel on its eastern side is dense with several rough footpaths that all branch off a main trail. The first time I ever saw the forest it reminded me of what the forest in Hansel and Gretel must have been like. The sky and daylight are effectively shut off while you are inside. I couldn't blame Katrine for not wanting to be here.

What person in their right mind would?

But if what Katrine's mother told me was the truth—and granted, that was probably a jumbo-sized *if*—then there were only a couple of ways into the forest from Chabanel.

Jean-Joseph was new to the area so it made sense he'd rely on Katrine for directions on how to get into the interior of the forest where there might be some kind of clearing suitable for a picnic. But from the few encounters I'd had with Jean-Joseph, he didn't strike me as the kind of guy who'd take a woman's advice for anything, and certainly not directions.

What is with Katrine? She definitely has a type—and it's not a good one.

With nothing else to go on except common sense, I rode Roulette to the first trail I came to that led into the woods. Coincidentally, I noted that this was also not far from the spot where I'd first met Deroy.

I hadn't spent much time thinking about what Deroy was doing in the forest or where he'd been coming from. The other side of the forest was at least ten miles away and as far as I knew there was only a highway and more pasture over that way. Another town or village would be somewhere in that area but where or how close I had no idea.

Once I reached the trailhead I slipped to the ground to get a better look at the path. I'm no tracker by any means but even I could see footprints in the soft dirt. As far as counting how many feet belonged to those footprints, that was well beyond my fledgling abilities.

My quickie assessment of the situation was that Jean-Joseph and Katrine were intent on finding a picnic-worthy spot so he could pop the question while a half-crazed, possibly inebriated Theo Bardot was following them.

I looked hard at the footprints. Surely I should be able to discern if a crowd of people came by this way recently? But to me it just looked like a bunch of kicked up dirt with the occasional possible boot print.

It occurred to me that if Theo had made it this far he would have left his bike nearby before going into the forest. But I didn't have time to scour every ditch and tree in the pasture by this section of the forest.

I swung back up into the saddle and squeezed Roulette with my legs. Not surprisingly, he didn't respond. This horse is a jerk on so many levels and the one where he thinks *he* should decide where he goes and how fast is my biggest issue with him.

I wasn't surprised he didn't want to go into the forest.

Hell, *I* didn't want to go in myself. I could already tell it was colder in there and dark and spooky.

But the last time I checked I was still the boss of this outfit and it was never going to be a good idea if Roulette thought otherwise.

I jerked his head up sharply and smacked his neck with the flat of my hand. Now before you start calling PETA or whatever, I can tell you I didn't really hurt him, but I *did* get his attention. The next time I gave him the cue to move forward he'd at least hesitate before outright refusing.

He snorted and tossed his head and then finally deigned to enter the forest.

The smell of pine and rotted wood hit me as we walked down the path. The trees instantly closed in around us so I could only see about twenty yards ahead of me. As expected, the canopy created by the overhead branches cut out most of the light.

The trail I was on was mostly mud and pine needles. Sound seemed to have deadened too. I heard the squeak of my saddle leather and the occasional sound of a chirping bird in the treetops.

The more we rode into the forest, the more nervous I felt. And so of course, the more that nervousness got transmitted to Roulette. As we penetrated deeper into the forest interior, I found myself imagining what Katrine must be feeling as she walked this way—hating every step she took.

Granted I was nervous and worried about Katrine and wondering where Theo was in all this but honestly even if I hadn't been it was hard to imagine how any sane person could think *this* experience was romantic in any sense of the word.

I was sure Katrine was being all tight-lipped and miserable about now. And I imagined Jean-Joseph was just self-absorbed enough not to notice.

Every once in awhile I stopped and tried to hear something besides the natural noises of the forest. But every time I stopped I only heard Roulette's snorts or the jangle of his bridle, the call of a bird in the trees, or the pounding of my own heart.

And every time I started moving again, I cursed Jean-Joseph and his idiocy that ever made him think this forest picnic was a good idea.

To combat my nervousness I started formulating a speech I imagined giving Jean-Joseph when I caught up with them: a speech about how he doesn't really know Katrine and if he did he'd never have insisted they come into the forest. In my mind, as I was giving this speech, I was seeing Katrine's eyes soften as she listened to me and began to realize how well I know her and how much I care for her.

So it was a warm and fuzzy daydream right up until the moment that Roulette stopped dead, flattened his ears and took two steps backward.

If you know anything about horses you know this is very unusual behavior and not in a good way. The alarm he was transmitting to me now throbbed in my gut. My first instinct was to soothe him and utter a few words of assurance but I couldn't get my voice to make noise.

Something had scared him. Something I couldn't see but that Roulette knew was worth being afraid of.

Giving in to my fears would only make things worse so I forced out a strong and steady voice.

"Whoa there, boy."

Miraculously, Roulette stopped moving backward, but his ears flicked as if he were straining to pick up whatever it was he'd heard in the first place. He whinnied loudly and I didn't blame him because by then I heard it too.

It was a groan.

Coming from the bushes straight ahead.

A human groan.

"Hello?" I said, gripping the reins tightly. "Who's there? Katrine?"

I could feel Roulette's muscles tighten beneath me like a coiled spring. Instantly I imagined him swiveling around and bolting back through the dense bushes and close-set oak trees—my kneecaps getting neatly severed in the process.

"Help," a voice said, thin and thready.

Hearing the voice gave me the focus I needed to act. And weirdly, my decisiveness seemed to calm Roulette. I slid off him and looped the reins over his head and quickly tied them to a nearby bush.

I took three steps off the path in the direction of where I thought I heard the voice. Three steps were all that were necessary.

He lay crumpled on his side, his knees brought up to his chest, a long ribbon of blood drizzling down from his scalp, his eyes closed tightly.

It was Jean-Joseph.

41

LIES AND LIARS

Luc stood in the apartment that Katrine shared with her mother Suzanne Remez. The woman—blousy and harried, clearly flustered at Luc paying her a visit—clutched a tissue in her hand where she sat on the worn divan in the room.

Katrine's two daughters, Babette and Odette, sat next to their grandmother, their eyes large with apprehension.

Madame Remez admitted that Jules had visited less than an hour ago.

"My daughter and Monsieur Dimer went for a picnic," Suzanne said, twisting the tissue in her hands. "Monsieur Dimer intends to propose to Katrine today. It is a happy day for the whole family."

"Where is this picnic to take place?" Luc said. "And when?"

"Well, I'm not sure. They left hours ago. Jean-Joseph had it all planned down to the last detail. He went to the *boulangerie* and even asked me for the heirloom engagement ring that belonged to Katrine's grandmother. Of course I was not able to part with that but—"

"*Where*, Madame Remez?" Luc said impatiently. "Where is this picnic to take place?"

Luc could literally feel the seconds ticking by—every one a possible death warrant for Katrine if Theo was as dangerous as he now believed.

"I think Jean-Joseph decided that they would go to the canal for their picnic."

"But Grandma," Odette said, "you told Madame Hooker that *Maman* went into the—"

"Shush, Odette! Let the adults speak." Suzanne turned back to Luc and smiled almost coquettishly. "I might have told Jules that Katrine and Jean-Joseph were going to the meadow beyond the mill for their picnic."

"No, Grandma," Babette said, "you told her they were in the fo—"

"Must I make you girls leave the room?" Suzanne said, her face cold and stern. "Not another word from either of you." She turned back to Luc and forced a brittle smile. "I suggested to Monsieur Dimer that he take Katrine to the canal for their picnic—it is so lovely this time of year—and I am sure he agreed that would be perfect."

Luc frowned. "So why did you tell Jules Hooker that they went to the meadow which is nowhere near the canal?"

Suzanne grimaced. "Surely that is obvious? I did not want her interrupting this most important moment in Katrine's life. My daughter has carried a heavy burden, Chief DeBray, these last few years. Ever since her first husband...went away...she has had to endure the humiliation of his many crimes."

Luc tried to remember if he'd heard that Katrine divorced Gaulter while he was in prison but nothing came to mind. Not that it mattered.

As far as Suzanne sending Jules on a wild-goose chase to

the meadow across town, at least that would keep her out of harm's way, he reasoned, until he or Matteo could apprehend Theo.

He glanced at his watch and worked to line up the pieces of the situation before him.

A man on a bicycle, even a seriously inebriated man—especially with a ferocious intent—could make it to the canal from the village in less than an half hour.

Theo had been gone for much longer than that.

It was easily enough time to have reached the canal by now.

Luc felt a sour taste in his mouth as he imagined Theo—very possibly a killer and certainly unstable at this point—as he intercepted Katrine and Jean-Joseph at the canal.

He cracked his knuckles and glanced at his watch again.

"Which section of the canal?" he asked, already moving toward the door.

Suzanne looked at him with bewilderment. "How would I know that?"

"The canal is fifteen kilometers long," Luc said in exasperation. It would take him the rest of the afternoon, even in a car, to scour every portion of its banks.

"It's very pretty this time of year," Suzanne repeated, almost defensively.

Luc hurried through the door, not bothering to close it behind him, his mind already computing the fastest way to reach the canal.

He didn't have a moment to lose.

If it wasn't already too late.

42

THE ONLY THING TO FEAR

I rushed to where Jean-Joseph lay, my thoughts racing around my head like dual-track speed cars.

What had happened?

But before I even reached him I answered my own stupid question.

Theo Bardot had happened.

I knelt by Jean-Joseph's side and touched his arm. His eyes flew open and he looked about as though he expected to see demons flying about the woods.

"Jean-Joseph, what happened? Where's Katrine?"

I looked around the flattened bush and the surrounding ground where he lay. Blood speckled the grass.

I was finding it difficult to swallow and my heart felt like a jack-in-the-box going off over and over in my chest.

Theo had Katrine.

"Help me," Jean-Joseph moaned as he reached out and grabbed my arm. "He tried to kill me."

"Can you sit up?" I asked, eyeing his head wound which looked to be still bleeding. I know medical stuff only from what I've seen on CSI but either Theo had given him a good one across the head with a baseball bat—unlikely in France—or Jean-Joseph had fallen and hit his head on something hard.

I eased him into a sitting position and sure enough there was a boulder behind his head coated in gore. It probably didn't matter *how* he'd gotten his head wound at this point. But there was no way Jean-Joseph could have done this on his own—and even less way that Katrine would have voluntarily left him when he did.

"Where is Katrine?" I asked again as I pulled out one of my handkerchiefs from my pocket. I wadded it up and pressed it to the back of his head.

He cried out and batted my hands away.

"I'm sorry, Jean-Joseph. I know it hurts. But you need to hold this to your head. Can you tell me where Katrine is?" I said more loudly, feeling the fear ratchet up in my throat until I wasn't sure I could breathe.

"Theo Bardot," Jean-Joseph said, taking the handkerchief from me and pressing it gingerly to his head. "He attacked us."

I looked in the direction of the path that curved ahead deeper into the forest and felt a sickening fluttering sensation in my gut.

"How long ago?"

"My head hurts so badly," he said. "I can't think straight."

"Did Theo...did he attack Katrine?" I licked my lips and prayed I wasn't going to find her body further up the trail.

"She ran," he said, closing his eyes against the pain and dropping the now blood-soaked handkerchief to the ground. "You have to help me."

She ran. And Theo chased her.

He clutched my arm. "I feel dizzy. Am I dying?"

I wanted to say *I have no idea* but even jerks are pitiful

when they're this afraid. I unplucked his hands from my jacket and got up to bring Roulette closer to him.

"I'm going to put you on my horse," I said as I unbuckled the near stirrup and dropped it several holes so Jean-Joseph could more easily mount up. "Can you stay on him without falling off? He'll take you to where you can get help."

"No, I need *you* to take me."

"Okay, well, I'm not going to do that. I need to go after Katrine and Theo so either you take my horse or you lay here and try not to bleed to death."

I could hear the impatience in my voice and a part of me was sorry about that. But the other much bigger part of me needed to catch up with Katrine and Theo.

I could literally feel the seconds ticking away in my head as with every one of them Katrine and Theo got further and further away.

"I'll fall off!"

"Then you're going to be much worse off than you are right now," I said. "My advice to you is don't fall off."

He blinked his eyes open wide and looked more alert to me. I think once he realized I wasn't going to baby him, a part of him woke up to do what he needed to do.

I'm not saying he was happy about it—he was a lot like Roulette in that way—but as his eyes flashed angrily at me, I could see he'd do his best to stay on.

"Grab the stirrup leather and pull yourself to your feet," I said. I snuck under his arm and felt him heave almost his whole weight onto me as he slowly stood up.

"Grab the stirrup!" I gasped, convinced I was about to fall to my knees any moment.

He finally did and the release of his weight nearly made me topple over. I went to Roulette's head and held his bridle.

"Put your foot in the stirrup," I told him, trying to keep

the impatience out of my voice. "Grab the saddle with both hands and haul yourself up. You can do it."

Grunting loudly, Jean-Joseph put his foot in the stirrup while I held Roulette steady. His first try he didn't make it and I forced myself not to curse at the time we were wasting.

I should just leave him in the bushes!

But I knew I couldn't do that. The second time, he managed to make it into the saddle.

I looped the reins under the cantle.

"Hold onto his mane, Jean-Joseph. Can you do that?"

I turned Roulette around, his head now pointing in the direction we came.

"I think I'm going to throw up," Jean-Joseph said.

"Do what you need to do," I said. "Just don't fall off. He'll take you to *La Fleurette*. If he gets going too fast for you..." I paused because I didn't really have any advice for him if that happened. He wasn't a good enough rider to impose his will over Roulette. My only hope was that if Roulette tried to pick up the pace going home somehow Jean-Joseph would be able to hold on.

Even if he made it within a couple miles of *La Fleurette* the twins and Marco would see the riderless horse and assume I'd been thrown and come looking for me. They'd eventually find Jean-Joseph wherever it was he landed—assuming of course he hadn't broken his neck in the fall.

I made clicking sounds and Roulette wasted no time in taking me up on the offer to leave. He moved at a fast walk back the way we had come.

Good luck, I thought as I watched them for the briefest of moments before turning toward the forest path and starting to run.

As I dodged sticks and brambles in the narrow pathway, I tried to figure how long it had been since Katrine and

Theo had come this way. I couldn't see any signs of clothing caught on the branches to indicate a pell-mell run but then I'm not sure *not* seeing these things meant she wasn't running for her life.

Because I'd spent so much time trying to sort out Jean-Joseph, I jogged for the first minute or two before allowing myself to stop, catch my breath and listen for any sounds that might tell me if they were near.

I could hear the thudding of my heart in my chest as my mind whirled in agitation.

Had Theo meant to hurt Jean-Joseph so severely? Was Theo in his right mind? If Katrine was still out here, why wasn't she screaming?

A feeling of dread slithered into me.

Had he already caught her?

Theo had long legs and he was fueled by anger and humiliation.

Katrine's only hope was to hide. No way was she going to outrun him.

Not for long any way.

As soon as I'd caught my breath and was ready to continue on, I heard the sound.

My stomach lurched.

What I heard wasn't human.

It was primal. Threatening.

And close by.

Fear crawled across my scalp and I jerked a hand out to grab a nearby tree as if that might support me.

The sound grew nearer and louder until with one last ominous shake of a bush the creature appeared.

A giant wild boar, its tusks razor sharp and pointed at me.

Its eyes were wild with fury and intent.

A gush of odor—manure, fur and musk—filled my nostrils as I stared at the beast. It stood directly in front of me on the path.

I couldn't move. All I could do was stare at the thing in disbelief and horror while fear clasped me like a boa constrictor—squeezing every possible option for action out of me.

My breath caught in my throat as I stared at the monster. And then it charged.

43

LAWD HAVE MERCY

I know I screamed but that's all I know for sure. It's certainly the only thing I remember doing to help myself in the face of certain death and for that I'm extremely embarrassed.

I mean. Screaming?

It was hardly going to turn the tide when dealing with a seriously pissed-off killer porcine.

This is the confused, hysterical nonsense that was rattling around my terrified brain in the handful of seconds I had as the beast came for me tusk-first.

Perhaps that's as good an explanation as any for why I didn't realize right away that the boar never quite made it to me.

You know how people who survive a near-death experience say that everything slows down? It was like that.

One minute I was watching the boar barrel straight for me, his knife-like tusks gleaming and his little piggy eyes locked onto my soft underbelly, and the next minute I was watching him plow snout-first into the ground in front of me.

He came to a stop inches from where I stood quaking.

But he didn't stop on his own. He stopped as the result of the one hundred and sixty pound man on his back.

And the gaping wound that suddenly erupted across his throat.

It was the smell of the blood more than anything else that finally snapped me out of my daze, effectively serving to remind me that this was not some horror movie I was watching in Techni-Color slo-mo but the real thing—a huge, hairy, smelly pig was gasping out its last breaths literally on top of my lime-green Seevees.

I collapsed to my knees—*not* what I wanted to do I can tell you—because now I was way closer to the smelly nearly-dead boar than I wanted to be. And eye to eye with my movie-star handsome stud of a husband who lay across the beast's back, his hand gripping a butcher knife as if ready to do it all again.

"Marco," I gasped, tears springing to my eyes.

In a flash Marco slid off the boar and reached for me. He half dragged and half carried me away from the carcass until I could crumple in a more convenient spot.

I was having trouble breathing and my hands were shaking as Marco knelt in front of me, his eyes worried and dark with concern.

"Take a deep breath," he told me. "It is dead. It can't get you."

I tried but I still couldn't breathe properly. I looked past Marco's shoulder at the mound of hairy carcass.

"I...I can't believe that just happened," I said, gripping Marco's hands tightly. "God, Marco. What if you hadn't come?"

Marco grimaced and wiped his knife on the knee of his jeans.

The relief of my close call seemed to surge through me and I closed my eyes and turned my face upward. There wasn't much sun reaching the interior of the forest where we were but it felt good to do it anyway.

Quickly I tried to shake off my nerves. Time was wasting and we had none of it to lose.

"Marco, listen to me. Theo attacked Jean-Joseph and left him for dead—and is now chasing Katrine. We have to find them!"

I struggled to my feet, deliberately avoiding looking at the dead boar on the path.

"Marco, we need to *hurry*. They must have gone down this path. You didn't hear anything before you found me, did you?"

Marco shook his head.

It was possible that Marco was a little more shook up from his confrontation with the boar than he was letting on. After all, it was quite a feat—jumping on a charging boar's back and slitting its throat. I swear, I didn't know Marco had it in him. But I was so grateful to discover that he did.

Marco continued to hesitate until I felt a fissure of frustration erupt in my chest.

Does he not understand the urgency?

"Marco, if you're thinking of bringing that boar back to *les soeurs* we can do that later, okay?" I took several steps down the path before I realized he still wasn't behind me.

In confusion, I turned to see him still standing next to the boar, his shoulders slumped as if in shame at what he'd done.

What the hell? Was he broken up at having killed the stupid boar?

It was in the space of my confusion and mounting frustration that I heard the noise that had been there in the background all along but my fear had blotted it out for me.

A humming or whimpering sound.

I whirled around trying to look everywhere at once.

"Marco, did you hear—?"

And then I saw her. Nearly hidden by the bramble of vegetation and leaves.

Katrine was crouched next to a tree stump, her hands bound in front of her. Her mouth was covered with a piece of bright orange duct tape.

My emotions veered from elation to sickening horror to see her like this. I ran to her, ripping aside the low hanging branches of a fallen beech tree in the process.

"Katrine!" I gasped, turning toward her. And then I tripped and skidded on my elbow and knees to land at her feet by the tree stump.

I twisted around to see what I'd fallen over...

... and looked right into the lifeless face of Theo Bardot.

44

SOMEWHERE OVER THE RAINBOW

I stared down at Theo. His eyes were closed but I thought I saw movement behind the lids. There was blood everywhere and I couldn't believe that I hadn't been able to smell it before.

Once I saw it, I couldn't stop smelling it—like sweetened metal.

Marco must have disabled Theo just in time, I thought.

I looked at Katrine who was looking not at me but at Marco. And her look of terror made me realize that she did not believe she had been rescued.

Not at all.

I followed her glance to Marco who was still standing by the boar and nudging it with his boot.

"Marco," I said, a feeling of dread inching up my spine. "What happened?"

He didn't answer.

I crawled over to Katrine but before I could reach her, Marco called out, "Don't! Don't touch her!"

Something in his voice made me stop. My back was to

him but if I turned around I suddenly wondered if I would see the Marco I knew or someone else entirely?

"Theo tied up Katrine, Marco," I said. "We need to hurry and—"

"He didn't tie her up," Marco said.

I looked at Katrine who squeezed her eyes shut as if the whole world was too much for her to endure another moment.

I stood up then, my stomach lurching, my brain on fire as if bells were clanging and ricocheting through my skull. I turned to look again at Marco. He stood staring at the dead boar. I saw the knife he'd used tucked into its sheath at his waist. I tried to remember if I'd ever seen Marco wear a knife. I cleared my throat and tried to get my thoughts in order.

Marco had stopped Theo before he could hurt Katrine.

But it was Marco who'd tied her up.

"Why?" I asked, my brain still refusing to put the pieces together. "Why would you do this?"

"You know why."

I stared at him, my brain struggling to put the pieces in the right order. I rubbed my hand across my face helplessly.

"Katrine *knew* you were sorry for what you did last summer," Marco said. "But she wouldn't forgive you. I could understand *Eloise* being a bitch but *Katrine* was supposed to be your best friend."

Someone must have betrayed poor dumb Marco a long time ago was all I could think at that moment.

My second thought was that this could all be sorted out. After all, Marco had saved Katrine from Theo. True, he'd tied her up afterward but everyone knew Marco was just a sweet blockhead. He was probably confused about…I searched desperately for some logical, believable explanation for what he'd done.

"How did you know she was in the woods?" I asked. "The last time I saw you you were helping Léa down from the roof."

If I thought calling to mind *les soeurs* would somehow jolt him back into some semblance of the old sweet Marco, I was disappointed. I watched his fingers flex near the knife he'd sheathed at his belt and felt my gut contract involuntarily.

"I came to the village looking for you," Marco said. "I overheard two old women coming out of the *boulangerie* saying Katrine and her boyfriend were going to the forest today for a picnic. I needed to shut Katrine up before she told what she knew."

I'd wasted so much time going to the city hall and then the police station and finally to Suzanne's place, that Marco had had plenty of time to race to the forest, intercept and disable Theo and prepare to punish the one person he felt had let me down.

Something was buzzing at the base of my mind like a fly that won't go away. Something important that told me I should be seeing something. But wasn't.

"Was it you who attacked Jean-Joseph?" I asked.

"No, that was Theo. He caught up with them and I guess he and Jean-Joseph fought. That's how I knew where they were. I heard them yelling. Then Theo punched Jean-Joseph, Katrine ran off and Theo ran after her."

"And so you ran after them and attacked Theo. So you saved her, Marco. That's a good thing. You're a hero." The words sounded false even to my ears.

Marco laughed. "Theo wasn't going to *hurt* her! He was *in love* with her! Didn't you know?"

"Marco," I said softly, hoping beyond hope that he was somehow still reachable, still the sweet Marco I'd known for the past five months. "I can't let you harm her."

"But she hates you!"

"No, Marco. She was just hurt and angry." I glanced at Katrine and saw tears streaming down her face.

"Well, it's too late now. She knows what I did."

"This was all a misunderstanding. We'll get help for Theo. Katrine won't say anything—"

Marco laughed. "Jules, stop! Katrine knows what I did!"

"Yes, but—"

He stood with his hands on his hips, his eyes not on me but on Katrine. There was something about *how* he looked at her—a manifestation of the finality of what he intended to do to her in spite of anything I said—that made the thought that had been teasing around the edges of my mind come charging into my head like a person who's been drowning and suddenly breaks the surface of the water, gasping for air.

"I needed to shut Katrine up before she told what she knew."

My stomach buckled as the truth hit me like a solid punch. In a flash I remembered how close Marco had been to me when I discovered Deroy's body.

Was it possible?

I nearly staggered at the realization. And as much time as I'd spent with Marco this week he never once even for one nano-second showed up on my radar as a possibility.

As if realizing what was going on in my mind Marco finally looked at me.

"I thought she saw me kill Deroy," he said with a half-hearted shrug. "She said she didn't, but it's too late now."

I moved to stand between Katrine and Marco.

"It's not too late, Marco. Help me get Theo back to the village. Come back with me. I will talk to Luc."

Marco snorted and flexed his fingers again near the knife. "Luc hates me."

"He doesn't hate you and he knows what you mean to me."

"That won't matter."

This wasn't going right. I now realized I had no idea what kind of person Marco really was and I was not at all sure I knew what to say to him.

"Why did you kill Deroy?" I asked.

"I saw him at the *fête* talking to Eloise. He kissed her. She was crying."

"And so you killed him?"

He shrugged. "I hate seeing Eloise cry."

Dear God, he's unhinged.

"I felt terrible about them coming after *you* for the murder, Jules. I never thought that would happen."

"But it was you who dropped my handkerchief at the murder site."

"That was an accident! Besides, I never thought they'd take you seriously as a suspect. I mean, you're dating the chief of police! You should have been totally safe."

"Marco, please," I said, hoping my voice wasn't shaking too badly. "I need you to give yourself up."

He slapped his hands against his knees and laughed. "The things you say!" He shook his head. "So serious!" And then he put one hand on his hip and his voice went up an octave as he said in a falsetto, sing-songy tones:

"*Trust me, Marco, I will prove you innocent of this terrible murder! Fabrice Charlevoix was a bad man but he deserves justice and you won't be the fall guy for Marguerite. I promise you!*"

Hearing my own words parroted back to me in his mocking tone wasn't nearly as bad as realizing what his words meant.

I'm slow. I admit it. It took me a full two seconds to understand what he was saying.

He killed Fabrice Charlevoix too.

I felt an urgent need to sit down but reached out to grab a nearby sapling for support.

"But...how could it have been you that killed Fabrice?" I said. "You were the one who came to tell me about the murder. And then...it was *you* who pushed Fabrice's body out the porthole?"

Marco grinned, his eyes glittering with merriment.

"Yes, of course. It was to make you think it was not me. Clever, no? Yes, Jules? You are surprised?"

I found my voice and wondered what in the world I could possibly say that would mean anything to this insane, depraved creature who'd I shared a home with for five months.

"I really, really am," I said weakly.

"Just like all the others you were always thinking you were so much smarter than me, but that's okay." He pulled the knife out of the sheath from his waist and turned to me. "After all, you are still my wife, no?"

"I can't let you do this," I said, backing up until I could feel Katrine's knees on the back of my legs. She was shaking violently.

"Except you can't stop me," he said easily, that old familiar Marco-smile slithering across his impossibly handsome face.

45

VOYAGE OF THE HEART

I lifted both hands up and stood my ground between Marco and Katrine.

"You're not thinking clearly," I said, noticing the flinch in his jaw as I said it. It wasn't until right then I realized that *poor dumb Marco* had probably chafed much more than I knew about how the world saw him.

This revelation didn't make him look any smarter to me, but hopefully I'd realized it in time not to make things worse.

"What I mean by that," I said hurriedly, "is that Katrine and I *both* know you killed Deroy."

He frowned at me, the knife still in his hand.

Honestly, what I was trying to say really depended on him not being willing to kill me too and that wasn't at all a sure thing.

"Except I know *you* won't betray me," he said.

"Okay," I said, preparing to walk across quicksand.

Holding a bag of venomous snakes.

"Because I've been so trustworthy before?" I said. "I betrayed Eloise, remember? And Katrine too."

That stopped him and while I knew this wasn't new information to him, I knew also that he'd pushed the reality of that away so he wouldn't have to look at it.

Somewhere in the back of the fog he calls a brain, Marco had already registered that I might not be totally trustworthy to my friends.

See how this approach could go sidewise in a hurry?

"You are saying if I hurt Katrine you will tell the police," he said slowly, piecing it all together.

"That's right. So unless you think you can kill me, too..." *Please don't let him think he can do that,* "I need you to put the knife down and not make things worse."

The silence that erupted between us made me realize that the whole damn forest had gone silent. Whatever birds or rustling in the bushes that had been evident before was totally gone now.

It was as if even the birds in the trees knew true evil when they saw it.

I could see by the way Marco stared at me, his face twisted in thought, that he was literally struggling with the question of whether or not he could kill me.

It occurred to me that now would not be a good time to throw up on my own feet.

"You betrayed Katrine," he said finally, "because you were trying to save a woman's life."

"What happened between me and Katrine was a spat like all sisters have. Hurt feelings. That's all. And because of who we are to each other, we *will* eventually make up."

Dear God, if you give us the chance to live past this day.

"And Eloise?"

"I'm sorry, Marco. There was no other way to get what I needed from Eloise but to lie to her. If it helps, I never really thought of her as a friend."

I saw his face brighten. "That is true. Not like you and me."

"Not like you and me, Marco. You and I are friends. So you're not going to hurt me—or Katrine either because that would hurt me greatly."

He frowned. "How can I just let you go?" The hand that held the knife lowered slowly to his side.

"Because you know we have to get Theo to a hospital," I said, praying I hadn't just pushed my luck.

Marco glanced at Theo's body on the ground. "Is he dead, do you think?"

"I don't think so but he will be if we don't get him help."

For a second I saw the indecision in Marco's eyes and I realized we weren't out of the woods yet. On the one hand, he was a cold-blooded killer, but on the other, Marco was still Marco. He was always going to prefer someone else make the hard decisions for him. I suddenly remembered that.

"If you were to continue down this path," I said pointing to where the trail went deeper into the forest, "you'll come out headed in the direction of Nîmes. That's a big city not too far from here and you can lose yourself there, Marco. Nobody will ever find you."

"Nîmes?" He glanced at Theo and then back at me.

"There's a refuge there," I said, "called *La Maison Carrée*. It's run by monks and they give sanctuary to anyone who goes there. You'll be safe there, Marco."

I saw him look at Katrine.

"If you hurt her," I said, my voice as cold and threatening as I could make it, "I'll tell the police what you did—and about the Marseille murder too."

When he looked at me, I saw no trace of the sweet gentle Marco I once knew.

"And if you decide that killing *me* will solve that problem for you," I continued, "then you should know that in that case you and all your descendants will burn in hell for all eternity."

I know that was probably a bit much even under the circumstance but I can only say in my defense that I was *really* stressed.

Marco blanched at my words.

"Go to Nîmes, Marco," I said firmly.

"I could never hurt you, Jules," he said sadly, a glimmer of hurt in his eyes that I could even think it. He hesitated for a moment longer and then re-sheathed his knife, his decision made.

"I'm sorry, Jules," he said.

"That's okay. No harm done."

Well, unless you count René Deroy and Fabrice Charlevoix.

"Will I see you again?" he asked.

"I'll find you at *La Maison Carrée*," I said, forcing a smile as I said the words.

"And this will all be like a bad dream," he said, his sweet Marco smile stretching across his face one last time.

"Hurry, Marco," I said. "*Run.*"

For a moment I thought he'd hug me goodbye and I prayed he wouldn't. Whatever I was able to make him believe with ten yards separating us I wasn't at all sure I could pull off if he touched me.

"*Je t'aime*, Jules," he said before turning and dashing down the path.

I went immediately to Katrine to work on the rope that held her hands. We were both shaking so badly that it took me longer than it should have to untie her.

When her hands were finally freed, she pulled the tape

from her mouth and without saying a word we fell into each other's arms.

46

AMERICAN PIE

Theo was too heavy to carry or even drag. I slapped his face lightly and his eyes fluttered open. He seemed to look at me before closing them again.

"That's a good sign!" I said.

"One of us needs to go for help," Katrine said.

I looked at her. She'd been through a lot and I wasn't at all sure she could handle making her way out of the forest in the dark.

Oh, did I mention it was twilight now? With no moon?

I looked at the darkened pathway that led out of the forest. I was pretty sure I couldn't do it either. I didn't have a flashlight and as soon as I stepped off the path I could easily be lost in the forest until morning.

And then there was the matter of roaming wild boars to worry about.

"You can't leave me, Jules," Katrine said as if reading my mind.

"I'm not leaving you."

Theo groaned and opened his eyes again. And then shut them again.

"We've got to get him help," I said. "He's had a head trauma. He can't just lay here all night."

"It's my fault he got hurt."

"How do you figure that? He was chasing you."

The tears began to trickle down her cheek again. "It's all my fault."

I left Theo and moved over beside Katrine and put my arms around her. It wasn't until then that I realized she was freezing. She'd come on her picnic with only a light cotton sweater. At least I was wearing a jacket. I slipped out of it and pulled it over her shoulders.

"What happened between you and Theo?"

She bent her head and I saw her shoulders shaking with her sobs.

"He saw me with Thibault last summer," she said finally, as her weeping subsided. "Thibault and I hooked up a few times. Nothing serious, just two people...needing to..." She waved her hand as if she couldn't find the words in the air.

"I get it. And Theo saw you with him. I guess he was jealous or something?"

She nodded. "I used to think there might be something between me and Theo. I got the vibes but nothing ever happened. After the thing with Thibault had run its course, one night I ran into Theo. It was late. He was drunk."

"Did he attack you?"

She nodded again, her eyes squeezed tightly closed.

"Rape?"

"Nearly. He came to his senses in time. But it was horrible. I ran off. And ever since then..."

"He's acted like *you* were the one in the wrong. Why is that, Katrine? Why did you let him make you think it was your fault?"

Katrine drew herself up straight and I watched her as she fought to gather her strength to answer my question.

"Something happened to me when I was sixteen," she said.

"A sexual assault."

"Yes."

I didn't know what to say to that so we sat in silence for a moment listening to the breeze whip the leaves in the trees. I glanced over at Theo. He'd shifted again before going still. Theo wasn't innocent. Not by a long shot. He'd made a terrible mistake but at least he'd recognized it and regretted it.

"I guess Theo felt ashamed about what he did," I said, "and that's why he ran against you in the election?"

"I guess. Ever since the night he attacked me he's been very aggressive toward me. It was like he could see I blamed myself and he wanted me to continue doing that."

"Is that why he decided to become the village drunk, do you think? Guilt?"

"He's been trying to apologize to me for weeks now. I just didn't want to hear it. I didn't want to remember it. I just…" Her hands fell impotently in her lap.

"You need to report what he did to Luc," I said.

Katrine looked at me in horror. "I could never! I just want to forget it."

"Can you really do that?"

Katrine glanced at Theo and after a moment she shook her head, another tear rolling down her cheek. "I don't think I can, no."

Right then was when I heard the rustle in the bushes and I flashed back to the memory of the killer porker attacking me at nearly this very spot.

I'm not proud of the fact that my first instinct was to

jump to my feet. I have no idea if I was thinking that I'd try to outrun the animal or wrestle it to the ground, but my heart was hammering so loudly in my chest that I couldn't hear a single other noise in my world.

So when my dog Cocoa burst out of the underbrush and hit me square in the chest, I fell backward onto my butt in a totally sound-proof world. Which was good because as soon as I lifted my head clear of the exuberant tongue-lashing by my deliriously jubilant dog, I could hear Katrine shrieking, "We're here! We're over here!"

Within ten minutes of Cocoa finding us, Katrine and I were sitting with steaming mugs of coffee spiked with brandy and huddled under very itchy wool blankets.

It seemed that Jean-Joseph *had* made it all the way to *La Fleurette* without falling off and was even lucid enough to tell Léa and Justine what had happened to him. Without Marco there to send for help the twins were in the process of stealing our neighbor Monsieur Moultier's bicycle when Adrien Matteo came by looking for me.

When *les soeurs* told him Jean-Joseph's story and how Katrine and I were in danger in the forest, the lieutenant hurriedly pedaled his bike back to town where, saints be praised, he was nearly run down by Luc in the car.

(Well, obviously, not saints be praised that Matteo was nearly run down. You know what I mean.)

Anyway, so Luc and Matteo raced back to *La Fleurette* where they spoke to Jean-Joseph who was nearly incoherent by this time but was at least able to deliver the important bits to them that needed relaying.

He and Katrine had gone on a picnic.
In the forest. Not the canal.

In my opinion Katrine's mother better have a darn good reason for why Luc shouldn't arrest her for obstruction of justice or whatever it's called. I'm just saying. Of course the idea of sending the police on a wild goose chase while your daughter was in mortal danger would be its own worst punishment for most mothers. So, yeah, I'm thinking Luc needs to throw her ass in jail.

Anyway, back to the rescue.

As soon as Katrine had shrieked our location to our rescuers, no fewer than a dozen people descended upon us—with the excruciatingly dashing Luc DeBray in the lead. Right after Cocoa finished cleaning my face with her tongue, Luc held me at arm's length to make sure I wasn't hurt and then crushed me so tight in a bear hug that I nearly fainted.

Matteo went to see what he could do for Theo and two men from the village materialized with a stretcher onto which they quickly loaded him.

The next part of the hour before Katrine and I were loaded up in Thibault's car—Matteo having used Luc's car to race Theo to the hospital in Aix—was an absolute blur but since I was warm and feeling no pain from the brandy, it was a very pleasant blur.

I'm not sure what Katrine was feeling because she was very quiet on the drive back. I suppose she was thinking of her girls and how close she'd come to never seeing them again. At one point Thibault reached out as he was driving and Katrine gripped his hand.

Luc sat next to me in the backseat and had yet to let go of me since the moment he'd come busting into the clearing with trumpets blaring.

I knew he was going to go absolutely ape-shit when I told him about Marco but I also knew that he was going to really love hearing it too. I didn't begrudge him that. Luc had never liked Marco and he'd been at least mildly vilified for that attitude because it made him look like a jealous jackass.

But is there anything worse than giving your boyfriend proof that he'd been right all along?

"Luc," I said, lacing my fingers tightly around his. "I know who Deroy's killer is."

He looked at me with surprise. "I do too. It's Theo Bardot."

And that's when I realized that there was plenty of time to tell Luc that Marco was the real killer.

I settled back into the car and basked in the fact that Luc was next to me with his arm around me. And that Katrine and I were both safe. And friends again.

And as we drove back to the village, safe and warm and alive, it occurred to me that I might have finally learned that when you really care about someone... all the rest of it just doesn't matter.

47
ONE MONTH LATER

Would it surprise you if I told you that four weeks after the last village festival, we were full swing into yet another one? This time it was the blessing of the bee hives—of which I think Chabanel has maybe two.

There were tables lining the village square groaning with baked goods, roasted meats, and also candles, jams and of course honey. It was going to be a lot easier to dance at this celebration, in spite of the cobblestones, and the usual amateur musicians were sitting with their guitars and drum sets making me especially sorry that we no longer had iTunes in our daily lives.

A lot had happened in the past four weeks, not the least of which was the fact that Katrine is now our mayor and has moved with her girls into the mayor's luxury residence in the center of the village.

I stood next to her on the square holding the hand of Odette while we watched two men fashion a wooden platform where we could all dance. Babette was still not too sure of me but I was confident I'd win her back over eventually.

Like her mother, Babette was an example that the good things took time.

From where I stood I could see Theo at the edge of the crowd standing in front of his café. He still has trouble with his vision and his memory. I'm not sure if that was the result of the hit on the head he took from Jean-Joseph or the beating with the tree branch that Marco gave him or all the drinking he had done in the months beforehand.

Anyway, after he got out of the hospital, Theo finally got his audience with Katrine—who remained resolute in her decision not to report his attack on her—where he apologized for what he'd done. He then resigned his position as mayor, which made Katrine the new mayor, and went back to running his café. He's currently looking for wait staff.

Katrine and I had plenty of time in the last few weeks to sort out our relationship. I figured her mother had been a wormtongue in her ear against me and I told Katrine I didn't blame her for not being nicer to me this summer if she could just forgive me for failing her during the election.

Amazingly, it seemed that in every real way Katrine had long forgiven me. She was just surrounded by people who didn't want her to be friends me. Now with Jean-Joseph gone—he moved on to a less exciting town—and Katrine's mother not invited to share Katrine's digs at the mayor's mansion—Katrine was ready to set her own course.

I knew, as Katrine did, that she had a habit of taking advice from people who were self-serving but she'd been burned a few times now and lost almost everything there was to lose.

If that doesn't knock some sense into you, I don't know what will.

Anyway, Katrine and I are back to being besties again. And something else good has come out of all this mess and that is that Thibault made it clear to her that he'd like to try again with her.

Now, I love Thibault to pieces but even I know that Katrine needs to take things slow. And maybe before she throws all her eggs in some guy's basket she might try carrying them around herself for a while first.

As for Marco, well, the revelation about him and what he'd done had a strong affect on a lot of people in the village, particularly me and *les soeurs*.

If you've ever seen the Disney movie *Beauty and the Beast* you might remember the part where Gaston is this handsome, virile stud-muffin who's in love with Belle but Belle wants nothing to do with him because he's a douche. The thing is though it's hard to remember Gaston is a douche because he's so cute.

See where I'm going with this?

When it came to Marco *les soeurs* were seriously put out with themselves—and of course with Marco—for having been fooled by him. I was particularly sorry about that. Normally, the twins have excellent radar when it comes to people but because they lived during the Nazi occupation they tend to lean in the direction of mistrust of new people. Hell, even of people they've known for decades.

I intend to keep a close eye on both of them to make sure they don't paint every stranger they came across with the Marco brush.

There are a lot of good people in the world and some of them I firmly believe we just haven't met yet.

With the banging of hammers in my ears, I looked past the stage construction site to see Luc step out of the police station. I gave Katrine's arm a quick squeeze to let her know I was leaving and then slipped away through the crowd.

I knew Luc had seen me so I wasn't surprised when after

I'd taken a quick turn by the goat pen—apparently there was some kind of goat beauty pageant as part of the bee hive festivities on tap for later—to find him standing there.

When I finally told Luc that it was Marco who'd killed Rene Deroy I have to say he didn't look at all surprised. Not that he suspected Marco for a single second but I guess there was some kind of deep and pleasurable satisfaction in knowing the guy you shouldn't hate was after all worth hating.

Marco, whose real name it turns out is Raol Ygraine was picked up twenty-four hours after he fled the forest. The directions I'd given him for *La Maison Carrée* was not a sanctuary at all but the venue for the semi-annual police convention taking place in Nîmes that week. I'd overheard Madame Gabin talking about it the week before.

Hey, it pays to eavesdrop. Don't let anyone tell you different.

As a result of the Franco-APB Luc had put out on him, the minute Marco walked into the convention—crawling with about two hundred fired-up police officers—he was immediately detained.

Marco promptly confessed to both murders that I knew of and another he'd committed several years ago that I didn't.

"Hey, Handsome," I said as Luc put an arm around my waist and drew me in close for a kiss. When I pulled away, I couldn't help but laugh.

"Is this the new Luc?" I said. I couldn't remember the last time Luc had even held my hand in public, let alone planted a big wet one on me.

"I think perhaps it is," he said mysteriously.

Luc had been pretty busy the last few weeks. First, he'd

had to let Eloise go because she'd gone totally batshit crazy and second, he'd been up to his neck trying to train her replacement, a pinch-lipped female clone of Adrien Matteo.

God, doesn't the police academy have any recruits with a sense of humor?

"Are you coming to dinner tonight?" I asked, noticing he still hadn't let go of my waist.

"Don't I every night?"

"Just making sure. Uh, Luc, is something up?"

"I cannot kiss my girlfriend on a public street?"

"Well, you never have before. Wait. You *are* talking about *me*, right?"

He grinned. "*Très amusant, chérie*. But I fear I have unsettling news for you."

Well crap. I knew the good times couldn't last long. Now what? Another EMP? Is the US declaring war on Europe? Is the truffle shortage not just a rumor?

"It appears that Marco, or rather Raol, married you under a false name." Luc's smile had faded and I felt a sudden chill in the air.

The looming presence of Grighot—just a few kilometers down the road—suddenly felt even closer.

"So I haven't been legally married all this time?" I asked.

"I'm afraid not."

"I see."

"May I make a suggestion?"

"I wish you would."

"How would you feel about being married to a policeman?"

I snorted and pulled away from him to get a good look at his face.

"Dear God! Is this a proposal or a game show question? I've waited a little too long for glib banter, Luc."

Luc grinned. "Yes, you have, *chérie*. My apologies." He dropped to one knee and held my hand to his lips, his eyes smiling at me with an intensity of emotion that defied words. "So?"

I will absolutely never forget that moment—the aroma of pungent goat poo wafting around us like a thick shroud peppered with the ambient sounds of braying donkeys, chickens and hopped-up screaming children.

And frankly I'll happily stack that moment up against the most ideal rose-garden proposal in the history of the world.

And by the way, that's a big fat *yes*, Chief DeBray.

Just in case there was ever any doubt.

ABOUT THE AUTHOR

Susan Kiernan-Lewis is the author of the bestselling *Maggie Newberry Mysteries,* as well as the post-apocalyptic thriller series *The Irish End Games, The Mia Kazmaroff Mysteries,* and *The Stranded in Provence Mysteries.* If you enjoyed *Wined and Died*, please leave a review on your purchase site.

To see sneak previews and giveaways as they happen, be sure and go to susankiernanlewis.com.